Keith Canty grew up in New York City, with his mother and eleven siblings. Despite his being from a low-income family, his mother Naomi Canty raised everyone to excel in school and pursue college if they wanted to pursue it. After graduating from Long Island University, Keith went into the social service field at various positions that include being a counselor, case manager, and the higher position as an intensive case manager. He worked with clients who were mentally ill, substance abusers, those on parole, and those experiencing other social conditions. Having once had his own apartment, Keith lost his position and those siblings he once assisted, betrayed him and forced him from his mother's home. He then entered the public shelter system, and experienced the multiple dangers, of why no one should ever have to live in a facility that supplies no assistance, and clients use every kind of drugs imaginable. He wrote this book as a warning to why every person should never ever consider living in the realms of a public shelter.

I dedicate this book to my mother, Naomi Canty, who taught me everything in life, to succeed, be independent, and much more.

Keith Canty

SIDES OF THE SAME COIN

From Employed to Homeless

AUSTIN MACAULEY PUBLISHERS™
LONDON • CAMBRIDGE • NEW YORK • SHARJAH

Copyright © Keith Canty 2022

All rights reserved. No part of this publication may be reproduced, distributed, or transmitted in any form or by any means, including photocopying, recording, or other electronic or mechanical methods, without the prior written permission of the publisher, except in the case of brief quotations embodied in critical reviews and certain other non-commercial uses permitted by copyright law. For permission requests, write to the publisher.

Any person who commits any unauthorized act in relation to this publication may be liable to criminal prosecution and civil claims for damages.

The story, experiences, and words are the author's alone.

Ordering Information
Quantity sales: Special discounts are available on quantity purchases by corporations, associations, and others. For details, contact the publisher at the address below.

Publisher's Cataloging-in-Publication data
Canty, Keith
Sides of the Same Coin

ISBN 9781649797582 (Paperback)
ISBN 9781638297819 (Hardback)
ISBN 9781649797599 (ePub e-book)

Library of Congress Control Number: 2021923281

www.austinmacauley.com/us

First Published 2022
Austin Macauley Publishers LLC
40 Wall Street, 33rd Floor, Suite 3302
New York, NY 10005
USA

mail-usa@austinmacauley.com
+1 (646) 5125767

I would like to acknowledge my special friend Dawn Michelle Burke for her assistance in not only helping with this book but also helping with my other multiple projects.

Chapter One
Ultimate Betrayal

My strange venture to being homeless began when I was evicted after losing my employment as a social service worker. I applied for many jobs after that, but the stain of losing a good job made it harder to obtain the employment that I sought. This and the fact that companies now had the luxury of selecting workers who worked for lower wages than what I worked for, made it even more difficult than what my employment and educational history demanded. Despite my assisting my mother, I was asked to leave my temporary residence at my mother's home, by former brothers and sisters that I had financially helped more times than I can remember. Such assistance included helping a postal worker, with a gambling predicament, repay his rent and move out of his apartment on a fourth of July holiday. Another incident included giving a dope-addicted former brother money to pay off his dope-dealing partners and prevent them from learning he had used the drugs he was supposed to sell. As wrong as this was, I thought my family ties made me obligated to assist him. Despite my assistance, I was quickly betrayed by them.

This same former brother is a jailhouse Muslim, who served time for manslaughter, and continues to use weed and other intoxicants routinely. This explains why he has the exact dope-fiend mentality and is ready to fight at the drop of a hat, as he had done years ago. Even after serving a lengthy jail sentence, he has yet to be rehabilitated, as his constant substance abuse, anger issues, and propensity for violence dictates. His anger issues often get the best of him despite maintaining a prestigious cleaner job that I assisted him to obtain. This same individual even threatened me and claimed that I insulted his son by refusing to allow his son to remain at my mother's home after he had stolen from her. My mother may have forgiven his ass but I for one, did not. It was bad enough that he stole from anyone, but to steal from someone who loved, helped raise, and trusted you, was not about to happen again. I simply did not trust him to live in my mother's home any time after that.

There were, of course, countless other times when my efforts and financial assistance was called upon, and freely given to those I once called family. This same generosity extended to those I adopted as honorary members of my family. One person I called cousin, was even a drug dealer, heroin user, bank robber, and spent years in prison when his mother was alive. I am bringing this person up because he helped evict me from my mother's home. This very person claimed to have found religion, only after his mother's death, yet he too betrayed me, and asked me to leave my mother's home for good.

The excuses that my now adversaries used against me were as comical as they were insulting. One brother had the nerve to say that the information they received from my mildly mentally impaired younger brother, was the reason why I was asked to leave. Keep in mind that all this was done without my, soon to be ninety-four-year-old, Alzheimer-ridden mother's knowledge. They made sure to have her taken outside the apartment by supposedly helping her to get some fresh air. I also firmly know that a conniving home attendant was in cahoots with this scheme. I overheard her discussing with my sister how they were going to change the front door locks and give everyone a new key except me. I also heard these people in secret discussions, in preparation for their asking me to vacate the home for good.

To prove the symbiotic relationship between this incompetent home attendant and my one-time family members, the following illustration reveals the true nature of their relationship. This home attendant was allowed liberties that went beyond anything outside of her assigned duties. My two former sisters lived in New Jersey, and sometimes took my mother to their homes for holidays, or long weekends. They and my brothers contently allowed this home attendant to enter my mother's home and call from the house phone to supposedly begin her workday, when they knew my mother was not present. This allowed the worker to make believe she started her workday at my mother's home, when in fact, she only called in from my mother's home, and immediately left the house after making such a call.

As I said, my family knew my mother was never home, and allowed this worker to abuse the employment call-in system that was implemented. In fact, this same postal working, ex-brother, would even call out from my mother's home for the home attendant, to make it appear that she worked the whole time at my mother's home. On other occasions, this same attendant was allowed to bring her two-year-old daughter, and her ten-year-old son, to my mother's home whenever they were out of school for holidays and vacation times. I spoke to agency officials and learned that this too was against all regulations. Keep in mind that this is the same home attendant, who also invited those same one-time siblings of mine, to her wedding in June of 2019.

In any event, the day I was requested to leave my mother's home, was without warning, assistance, and my having all but eight dollars in my pocket. As the conniving group of individuals hovered around and made sure I took the small amount of clothing that belonged to me, I could hear them whispering how they needed to make sure that all the locks were changed in case I somehow managed to make a copy of the key that belonged to my brother Billy. This information could have only come from the lying home attendant, who saw me enter the home when she failed to lock the door, after taking her time to answer it, when I was locked out.

As I left the home, the looks of sheer satisfaction on their faces, and the silent approvals showed me where this group stood regarding me. As much as I hate to say it, the deed that was done by them was as despicable, cold, and heartless as anything I experienced in life, and it was something I never expected to experience. They all felt they were administering a punishment that I would never recover from. Not only did they know I had no place to go, but they absolutely did not care what would become of me once I left. I was never a vengeful person, but for this offense, they all needed and deserved to be punished. Even the sister, who had stopped speaking to me months ago, looked on, and said nothing to defend me. This very sister, whose child I routinely picked up from daycare when my mother was incapable of walking such a distance, did not defend me. This further proved that she too wanted this to happen. I saw the glee in her eyes when this fake cousin relayed her sick message to me about making sure I returned my mother's front door key.

I grabbed my one large bag, that was heavy, but I also grabbed my laptop computer, and took it along with me. As I left the building, not one of my ex-family members gave me a hand, or even offered cash for bus or train fare. I knew then that they were all not part of my life anymore. For good measure, that fake cousin tried approaching me, and asking if I wanted to turn over any house keys because I did not want to cause any problems. I told that triple-faced person that I am not turning over a damn thing. Being the lowlife that he was, he quickly reported what I said to the rest of them, and I did not care. My last words to all of them were that I will undoubtedly see them again when they least expected it.

The clothing bag and my laptop were so heavy that I could barely manage to move them more than few feet at a time. Each few steps resulted in my having to stop and rest for lengthy periods. Even when I put the bag strap over my shoulders, it began to cut each limb until my forearms and shoulders became raw, red, and painfully sore. My plan was to save as much money as I could; so, a journey to the train station that would have normally taken me fifteen minutes, took me close to four hours. It took another hour to make it upstairs to the upper-level platform of the overhead downtown train. Once I boarded the train, it was well after the rush hour, but I was grateful that the Creator was with me and helped me get through this ordeal.

I got off at the train stop closest to the assessment center for homeless individuals. Making my way to the assessment center from the subway was a lengthy walk but carrying the load I was transporting was as backbreaking a chore as I could have ever done. I forcefully departed my mother's home at 4:30 pm that afternoon and I reached the assessment center at 11:30 pm that night. I was tired, sore, and hungry by that time, and all I could think of was that smug expression, on the faces of my one-time family members who took part in making me homeless. The look on the faces of those I once loved, and cared for, would never again be the same experience.

At the assessment center, it was hours before those waiting to be assessed were ushered into two different waiting rooms and were then told to wait until our names were called. It was another few hours before staff gave out lunch bags of food to eat. By that time, my hunger had gotten the best of me, and I cobbled down the jailhouse sandwiches, pretzels, and juice that shelter staff provided. Most people there were used to being homeless. Some talked about how many times they were in shelters, while others hoped to be transferred to facilities where their friends were located. Many ate the distasteful food as if it were gourmet meals. Others used the hard, stationary seats as beds and slept until staff called them hours later for transport to other facilities. I was one of the lucky ones who were given a bed and asked to return to this very department the next day as if my spending more than six hours here was easily not enough.

I dragged my bag, that was too heavy for me to lift anymore to the nearest elevator and made my way to the specified room that was assigned to me. Because the floor had signs that read *dormitory is just beyond this point*, I took precautions to make sure no one could enter the room where I was, without waking me up. I put the heavy, mental bed against the door and dared anyone to try entering when I was there. I worked in mental shelters before, and I knew some of the unfortunate things that happened at facilities like this. I was going to make sure nothing would happen to me. Despite the heavy police presence at the facility, they simply could not be every place at once. While the police and private security tried to do an admirable job, protecting everyone in this huge place was simply impossible.

My instincts and social service experience would again prove to be correct. During the middle of the night, someone tried entering the room by pushing the door and I awoke instantly. My street-mentality mode took over and I told the person to get his ass away from the damn door. The person immediately left without saying a word. The average person would have said, "Excuse me," or said, "My mistake," but because this person said nothing and simply tried entering a clearly marked door, I had a strong suspicion that this person was up to no good. The fact that I would wake up at the slightest sound was something that I developed during my early childhood. I slept quietly the rest of the night, without incident.

The next morning, I awakened before sunrise, and made my way down the hall to where the bathrooms and the showers were. I immediately noticed the clear scabs on my shoulders and left forearm, as if someone had taken a razor blade and peeled back blotches of skin that was all gone. This was easily the result of lugging my heavy bag and laptop with me for hours. I got dressed and made my way back to the intake assessment unit and waited until someone called me hours later. I was called to a woman's office, and she introduced herself as Ms. Zobee. Our initial discussion started with my completing forms that requested information like my name and educational level.

Ms. Zobee requested information on how I became homeless and was surprised that I even had a higher level of education and work experience than most clients that came her way. She looked over my information, and jokingly said that she was positive I could easily perform the duties of any worker not only in her department, but throughout the whole facility. I for one knew she was positively correct. Once she had the necessary information for her intake assessment, I was told to again go to the waiting area, and that someone would contact me. Two hours later, clients were again offered lunch bags like before. I ate the fruit and put the chips into my heavy bag for later. I was then given more papers and was told that I would be placed on the seventh-floor men's dormitory where I would see Ms. Smith.

I dragged my belongings to the elevator and got off on the seventh floor. While there were police at the entrance of the facility, they were not present throughout most of the areas in the facility. In fact, most of the facility was manned by security guards, who had the attitude that they remained safe and called the police whenever violent incidents occurred. I reported to the bed assignment office for the floor and was told the direction of the ward where my bed was located. After dragging my belongings down the hallway, I saw a lock on the locker that was assigned to me. I then dragged my property back to Ms. Smith's office and explained the situation.

Ms. Smith informed me that although the client had officially left, she had to first give the client a chance to come back to the facility and claim their bed. Just when it looked like I would have to lug my belongings again, Ms. Smith stated that she would not leave until 4:00 pm, so I could leave my belongings in her office until then, and her co-worker would cut the lock off the locker for me. Six hours later, I made my way to retrieve my belongings, and I thanked Ms. Smith for holding them for me. I was then told to report to the night supervisor's office and speak with Mr. Ross. I again dragged my belongings down the long hallway and showed Mr. Ross my bed assignment. I explained that I also needed the lock of the now former client, cut off the locker, so I could use it. I was then given another surprise by this supervisor.

Mr. Ross informed me of the agency's policy of giving a client until 10:30 pm to return to claim their bed. I now had another six hours to go before they could legally cut the lock off the locker that was supposedly assigned to me. I told Mr. Ross that he had got to be kidding, and that my arms were tired and sore as hell. Mr. Ross informed me, that what he could do is allow me to keep my belongings in his office, and I could retrieve them at 10:30 pm. At that time, a co-worker would do his client count for the night, and I would have the lock cut off the locker. While this was not the best solution, anything that would prevent me from having to drag my stuff around was good news to me.

I patiently waited for dinner to start and took the elevator to the appropriate floor where the cafeteria was. I waited in line with the other clients, as security officers looked on, to make sure no one jumped the line. I was given a temporary meal ticket that allowed me to enter the facility, and to eat meals whenever they were served. After having dinner, I then went to the seventh floor, and circulated from the television room to a waiting room, that had no working television, but allowed clients to sit, socialize, or keep to oneself. This was part of my assessment plan for anyone I ran into. It was easy to spot those who chose to make this place their new home and accepted the living conditions they were under. I had no intention of ever making such a place my permanent residence.

Hours later, the bed check was announced over the loudspeaker, and everyone had to be near, or on their assigned beds. I spoke to one of the security officers, who showed me the staff member that was assigned to cutting locks off client lockers. After speaking with this individual, I waited until it was time for all clients to go for bed checks. At the assigned bedtime, all lights were turned out, and clients were supposedly asleep. I waited in the darkened room for staff to arrive. Around 11:45 pm, this person finally came around, and cut the lock off my assigned locker. The staff had the nerve to tell me, that I could have taken the dirty sheets and blanket off the bed while I was waiting for someone to cut the lock from my newly assigned locker.

After the worker stripped the bed, I then put clean sheets on the bed, and I finally put my belongings into the locker, that I could temporarily call my own. I lay in bed as another client told the staff that had he known I was waiting to have the lock cut off the locker, he would have informed me of my being able to take the old sheets off the bed a long time ago. I did not know this client, but I clearly knew his type. His dark ashy skin, discolored eyes, and dope fiend thinking, told me all I needed to know about this substance abusing idiot. I also knew a suck up when I saw one, and I despised him for being that as well. I clearly knew this client was pulling game, and I knew he was not to be trusted.

I put my belongings in the locker and made sure to lock up the laptop that I had been carrying ever since leaving my mother's home. I finally got into bed well after midnight and took the rest that I surely needed. My thoughts raced from the conditions of these new surroundings to the betrayal I experienced from my family. It was at this time that I felt angrier than anything I knew before. I kept thinking about those, that I helped countless times, now making this nightmarish scenario a physical reality that I would never forget. It was during this time, that I understood, that certain family members, would no longer have the right to address, or speak of me as a family member ever again. This was not a simple argument or family disagreement. This was a betrayal that could never be easily forgiven. This was action that no amount of forgiveness could make right. I decided that I would never again associate with them, or ever allow them to be a part of my family ever again. Some may believe that it is impossible to disown family members, but for me, this was clearly what I decided to do.

Chapter Two
Life as a New Client

I awakened as the morning sunlight shined in my face the next morning. I then decided to shower while my follow clients were still asleep. I figured this would be the best time to enter the shower before anyone awakened and created a huge traffic jam to use the facilities. I knew where the showers and the bathroom were, from having spent yesterday exploring the floor level. I never liked the idea of having to rush, so I decided to take a shower, while most people were still in bed. While the showers close to where I was had two stalls available, I only had to wait until two people were through using them, before I was next in line. While most people were generally willing to reserve judgement on a person they did not know, it was not long before my street mode mentality was again needed to address an issue that was unexpected.

I was looking at the shower stalls, to see who was finishing, and this big, fat guy looked at me and asked, did I mind? I knew what he meant, but I was not in the mood to listen to him. I replied, what was it that he wanted me to mind? He then said that I keep staring at him, and he wanted to have privacy. My street mode kicked in at a higher level, and I instantly told him, who the hell wants to look at his fat sloppy ass, and I was waiting for him to finish showering, so I could use the facilities. Once he saw that I simply did not care, just like him, he cooled out and quickly finished. The person that was before me was so taken aback by my stance that he did not mind if I showered ahead of him. I politely declined, and rightfully let him take his turn before I showered.

I made my way back to my room, and some of the other clients were just awakening. A couple of them introduced themselves, while others slept, or kept to themselves. The one thing I noticed about this facility was that it had female clients, as well as male clients here. I made my way to the fourth floor, and again waited in line to eat. As I noticed before, security guards were on every floor, and they were generally helpful. Clients were also given positions in most departments, which made me question whether clients had any intention of ever leaving this facility anytime soon. Most clients become so comfortable with making income that they often refused to leave. The fact that some clients had positions for months at a time convinced me, they were indeed too comfortable being here.

There were a couple of people, whose positions where to clean the eating areas, after every meal. Two of those clients were also primetime shop lifters, who stole everything under the sun, and brought it back to the facility to sale. They then sold these products at reduced prices to other clients on the wards. One fast-talking guy named Mitch would dress up in an olive-colored dress suit, and travel to a large department store. This client would then pretend to scan items at the self-serving cash registers and slip these items into his bags without paying. Because he did not look, or dress, like a perceived shoplifter, security guards did not notice him. To this very day, he has so far, never been caught. Just about every evening, Mitch would display the products he stole to other clients and sell them at a huge discount.

I have seen clients selling chocolates, colognes, new clothing, cigarettes, snacks, portable fans, and a host of other items. It is for this reason that made me determined not to remain in this facility long and obtain my own place. The other reason I did not want to remain here was the fact that many staff knew people like Mitch were selling stolen items, and not only refused to do anything about it, but allowed them to remain employed at the facility. The social service worker in me would have easily addressed this issue long ago. My solution would be to let people like Mitch know that if he ever stole anything else, his job would be forfeited. On top of that, I would let these people know that I would then report them to the police, and the store they stole from, and have them investigated for shoplifting.

Nevertheless, my plans included getting out of here as fast as I could. This may have been a bold prediction for someone with no job and only eight dollars in his pockets, but I have always been a big believer in my abilities and what the Creator can do. After asking around, I found out that the only way to move from the step one, where I was, to step two was to complete an evaluation by the case manager. Since I spent years being a case manager, I knew this job like the back of my hand. I now had to go about finding one in this facility. I learned that most of the clients here had never completed step one, because many of them wanted to remain here to do their dirt and because it was comfortable for them to do so. I also knew that some workers knew when clients avoided them and did not care to engage them. I took it upon myself to find the case manager that I needed.

I first needed to learn how these case managers were assigned to clients. As I said before, at one time, I was a case manager, so I knew such assignments are given out by the supervisor of the unit. I made my way to the case management supervisor and introduced myself. I then asked if it would be a problem if she assigned a case manager to me. The supervisor seemed taken aback by the question and looked at me silently for a few seconds. She then asked me to come back at 2:00 and sign a sheet she will have taped to the back of her door. This list will be for a list of new clients that are assigned to case manager named Ms. Baily. She then said that she would alert Ms. Baily that I was now on her case load. That sounded easy enough, and I still could not understand why so many clients refused to do what I just did. I could not understand if this were because of my professional experience or because she knew I was not as gullible as the other clients she was used to.

I returned, at the scheduled time, and Ms. Baily was finishing up with a client. She interrupted her session and introduced herself to me. She said that I could wait for her in the waiting room across the hall and she would come get me in a little while. I took a seat across the hall and learned more about how some clients were occupying their day. Many clients had state cell phones, and played music, and games throughout the day. I listened to clients talk about how they routinely snuck off grounds after curfew to use the drugs they purchased to get high or make money from other clients. As I was educating myself to the habits of others, Ms. Baily entered the room and asked me to come to her office.

After I entered, she offered me a seat and explained the procedure for getting out of this shelter. She also explained how my next shelter would assist me in obtaining placement into a permanent facility, or a place that would help me pursue independent housing. Under normal condition, my finding an apartment would be child's play, but with no income coming in, and only eight whole dollars in my possession, I needed to utilize every avenue I could find. Until I found employment that could enable me to pay the rent that I was used to paying, my only other options were low-income housing, and my being in the shelter system made me a prime candidate. I soon realized that every worker I spoke to has the required duty of first completing an assessment on every client. Ms. Baily was no different the other workers.

After giving my slandered answers to how I became homeless, Ms. Baily became intrigued about my employment and my college education. She became more captivated when she learned that I initially went to college under a basketball scholarship, and took music classes, and was then awarded a scholarship for music. Once I told her that I also had a bachelor's degree and a multitude of certificates in social services, she went completely over the top. She said loudly that she knew there was something unique about me that separated me from other people. She became so bewildered that she could not believe that such a person like me could end up in a homeless shelter system.

Ms. Baily's attention then moved to how I spent much of my free time since coming here.

I explained that I was basically a loner, and when I was not dodging the weed pushers, dope dealers, and pill poppers, most of my time was spent on writing books, screenplays, movies, and television scripts. The more I talked about my interest and plans, the more intrigued she became. She stated that she thought I had the potential to one day be extremely successful. I told her about two of the five books that I had written called *Through Less than Perfect Eyes*, and *Social Service Pimps—the Whoring of the Mentally Ill*. She said that she is an avid reader, and she knew that these books would do well on the book market once they got into stores. She was also thrilled by the possibility of my stories hitting the television and movie screens around the country, if not the world.

I then shared my sympathy for her because I knew her job must be difficult with these extremely large caseloads and having so many clients who are substance abusers. She nodded her head in agreement before asking, would I mind if she confided in me about something. I told her it was alright to confide in me, especially since I had been in her shoes. Ms. Baily then stated that her caseload was far too large to manage, and many clients avoid completing their assessments, because they know that would keep them from moving to other facilities. She then said that she had no doubt that I would do well in life, and I would not be in this facility long. After a lengthy discussion, Ms. Baily saw the clock and knew it was time to meet with her supervisor. She then said that my assessment was nearly done, and we could easily meet tomorrow for fifteen minutes and finish up. I was eventually given an appointment for emergency food stamps and a Medicaid card for that Monday.

I wanted to get some air, so I took my laptop and made my way to the public library that was down the street. I checked my emails, started to write another book, and headed back to the facility for dinner time. I showed my meal ticket that allowed me to reenter the facility and eat the meal that was being served. I watched intently as most con artists, drug dealers, and shop lifters, all had paying positions at this facility. Even those who were non-compliant with case managers were routinely hired as if their services were vital. I later returned to the seventh floor and stayed in the television room until bed check was called. That night, I received another surprise. I did not have any friends in this place, or any other facility, so I was surprised that someone approached me.

The same drug-using client, who slept a few beds down from me asked everyone in the room to meet with him for a few minutes. I initially said no because I recognized the look in his eyes and knew that he was as high as a kite. Another client who was intimidated by this drug user asked if I could please hear what this client had to say, so he could shut the hell up, and we could go on about our business. I agreed with that sentiment, and we let him say his piece. As I approached this client, he said his name is Reese, and he wanted us to know that he uses just about every drug under the sun, and if we ever needed anything to get high, we should let him know and he would get it for us. I told Reese that I did not get high, so I basically did not care what he did. Reese then said that he needed to make sure that no one would rat him out to staff. He then asked if I could look at something he needed to show me in his locker. I escorted him to his locker, and he showed me various pills, drugs, and concoctions, that many drug users here craved.

Once he saw that his plans were not tempting me to agree with him, he resorted to another route. Reese said, that since we all live together, he would like to take us all out to eat, and just have a good time. I again declined the offer, and he continued to insist. He went on about how another client here is his true friend, who also gets high with him. I again explained that while I have no issues with him personally, I do not get high or socialize with anyone on drugs. Reese argued that sense we will be living together as a group, we should get along. I explained to Reese, that so long as he kept his poison away from me, we will be alright. Seeing that his tactics were not working, Reese then said, that today was his birthday, and he is going out to celebrate as soon as the staff did their client bed checks for the night. I wished him a happy birthday and left it at that. I also had doubts that it was even his birthday. While I lay in bed, I saw Reese leave the room about an hour after bed check. I shook my head and thought this has got to be a waste of life. I knew I would be addressing his dope-fiend ass later when I got the chance.

The next day, I was called into the weekend supervisor's office to discuss something. The supervisor told me that a bed was available at another shelter, and I was to be there before 10:00 pm today. I explained that this was really a quick transfer since I was not even there two whole days. The supervisor said that I should be proud of that, because now I will have the chance to move to level two, where priority will now be given to addressing my housing needs and moving to my own place. I was then asked if I wanted to eat dinner before I left. I declined this offer, and asked the supervisor, can he say goodbye to Ms. Baily for me. He wrote a goodbye note and put it on her desk. I was given travel directions to the shelter I was transferred to. Luckily, I only had to drag my property one block, and take the bus. I arrived at the new shelter, just after 10:00 pm, and my life as an official new client had just begun.

Chapter three
Learning the Ropes

At no point in my life did it ever occur to me that I would one day have to adjust to life inside a homeless shelter. With my high income, I never envisioned myself needing the assistance of shelter officials, but the circumstances dictated otherwise. Despite my dilemma, my optimism for life made me believe everything would turn out alright. I recited positive affirmations, sighted optimistic promises to myself, and prayed every day that this nightmarish reality would soon be over. I even told myself that I would one day look upon this venture in life, and somehow be amused. I should have known better when I faced a familiar situation as I did in the last shelter. It seemed that the locker that was assigned to me still had the lock on it. I was again prevented from storing my belongings. As I waited hours for the staff to address this lock situation, a support worker finally came around, and asked another client, to use the key in his possession to open the lock. As a reward for the client's assistance, the staff allowed this client to help himself to any personal hygiene products, and valuables that were previously left in the locker.

I put the new bedding on the bed and placed my belongings in the locker that was assigned to me. Once the staff left the floor, clients turned on personal night lights, and talked freely amongst themselves. The topic of conversation included the usual ignorant topics of who was getting high, who owed which person money, and how certain products could be sneaked passed security. My experience as a caseworker let me know that I had to meet with the intake worker and let him do his assessment on me before I could be assigned a case manager. I knew this person would have no problem in seeing me, because I was different than his other clients. Many clients did not care to whether they stayed in the shelter or not, but I was determined to be compliant, and get out of here as soon as possible. I learned the intake worker's name was Mr. Holmes, so he became my immediate target.

I staked out Mr. Holmes's office the next day and let him know that I needed to meet with him immediately. He initially tried giving me the story about being patient, but I was not hearing that, and explained that my assessment would not take long. We agreed to meet that afternoon, and he even called me into his office earlier because another client did not show up for their meeting. After seeing the previous assessments homeless service staff did on me, Mr. Holmes saw this as an easy cut and paste matter to complete his assessment. He saw that my situation was a matter of circumstances, and my work history included performing every duty that he was performing. We wrapped up our session within minutes, and he said that I should give the case management team a day or two before they assigned me a case manager. I was not interested in waiting. I made myself known to the case management team and told them that I could make their jobs easier. The next day, I was asked to meet with Mr. Baszler, my newly assigned case manager.

I began to do my own assessment of things in this facility, like I did the last facility. Just like I saw that most of the clients were given jobs, many of the clients here were ex-convicts who were now on parole and had to report to their parole officers consistently or be violated. In fact, some clients even had lifetime probationary periods that subjected them to immediate incarceration if they did anything illegal. Probably the most difficult thing I faced was getting accustomed to the jailhouse mentality that most clients had. While I knew that getting accustomed to this environment would take some getting used to, there was no way in hell that I was going to accept these conditions, that were just steps below a jailhouse penitentiary. For every meal, each resident had to tell an on-call security officer their bed numbers and get in line to eat. On top of that, clients had to again give their bed numbers to assigned workers before going to bed or risk losing their beds once bed checks were done. Furthermore, each client had to be in or near their beds when nightly bed checks were done, otherwise they would lose their assigned beds.

It was easy to see, that even the security guards had little dedication to their positions. Some worked hard and tried to make a difference, while others complained constantly about other workers and aspects of their jobs that they could not stand. I heard one officer complain that contraband is brought into the facility regularly, and nothing is done about it. One recent officer was complaining that some guards do not do anything when they know clients are smoking weed in the dormitories. Some staff even treated clients as if they were their very friends, and often overlooked infractions that others would be violated for. In fact, one morning I was standing at the entrance of the facility, when a guard, who knew I lived here, started a conversation with me. I found it odd because he had never spoken to me before. Out of the blue, he said that I should get into the habit of always signing in at the front desk, in case the parole department came by, and checks to see if their clients were on the grounds and violate them for not being here.

I informed this guard that this stipulation had nothing to do with me, because I had never been in trouble with the law, and I was not on probation or parole. This officer then stated that I should still make it my business to sign in anyway, because the probation department is making a fuss about it. I knew he was not making any sense, but I just went on about my business anyway. I personally did not care what the parole department thought of me because they had no jurisdiction over me. Later that day, I spoke to another client who got out of jail within the past few months, and he told me, that he knew several of the security officers, and support staff who used to be inmates with him. I found that to be amazing that former inmates are now employed at this facility. In any case, I was now meeting with my assigned case manager in less than three days.

My case manager was out of college for about a year, and he was basically learning the job on the fly. I shared a secret with him that I worked at this very agency, for a total of nine days before quitting, and doing something else. I let Mr. Baszler know that I fully understood how overworked he was, and that my caseload was well over fifty clients when I worked here. Mr. Baszler confessed that his current caseload was well over fifty-three clients. Mr. Baszler reviewed my employment history and was extremely impressed. He mentioned that he did not particularly like his position here, because others had told him negative things about this agency, and the people that ran it. After discussing my background, and future, he too came away overly impressed, and said there was no way I would remain homeless or jobless very long.

Mr. Baszler also said that he too had plans to move on from here as well. I explained that that would be to his best interests because most clients here simply do not want to be helped. Mr. Baszler understood that while most here do not care one way or the other, there were a few that he intended to help. I gave him information on state positions where he could apply for jobs and make an excellent salary. He promised he would be investigating those positions as well. He also said that he intended to assist me in getting out of here as soon as possible. I lastly informed Mr. Baszler of my intentions of starting a program for homeless individuals who want to make their lives better. He wished me luck and said he would be glad to refer needed clients to this facility once it was established. I was not sure whether he intended to truly assist me, or he was just amusing me, but I decided to give him the benefit of the doubt and see.

We also got into a discussion regarding my vocational interests. Ms. Tames, who was an employment instructor, came to our site, and informed clients of the multitude of jobs, and employment trainings they had to offer. I was reluctant to trust this type of training because the setting for her presentation was very much to be desired. I was in the cafeteria during dinner time when she arrived. Clients were busy eating their dinner, talking, while others were yelling out their bed numbers to the security staff to be checked accordingly. On top of that, the television was blasting, and anyone could hardly hear anything that was being said by Ms. Tames. I did manage to hear that such training programs included security guard training, catering, and maintenance, along with other duties clients looking for a work could get into. Despite my apprehensions, I called and spoke with Ms. Tames by telephone and expressed my interest in her program. Ms. Tames, stated that I should come in to see her this coming Monday morning, so she can further explain the program and do my assessment.

Keep in mind that these assessments were not difficult to do at all. As I said before, most of the work was simply cutting and pasting information from one assessment to the next, with a small addendum by the new worker. The workers just logged on to the agency site, added a sentence or two of their own, and the assessment on a client was easily completed. Since every client was already in the computer system doing such assessments was merely child's play. I arrived at the vocational site at 9:00 that Monday morning and waited for Ms. Tames to arrive. Twenty minutes later, security guards informed me, that Ms. Tames had arrived. It was well after the scheduled time that we were supposed to meet, but I was patient. Minutes later, a security guard told me that workers were just getting in, and they needed a few more minutes to get into their work mode. Every job I ever worked, dictated, that you be prepared to start workday the minute you arrived at the site, but this place was by far, different than anyplace else in terms of unprofessionalism.

Twenty minutes later, I was asked to come to another room. As an assistant gave me identification, and work experience papers to complete, I could clearly hear the security guard training taking place in the next room. I heard the instructor leading the class in a chat that went, we are good, we are getting hired, and we will do greatly. I put my pen down, and could not believe this amateurish nonsense, that I was hearing. As the class continued to recite this nonsense, I saw the instructor go into another room, and ask his co-worker, did she hear his class chatting? He then said, they are getting the message, and that he was breaking them down, and building them back up again. This was the most absolute example of nonsense I have ever witnessed. I had no interest in such participation. It would have been amusing had the situation not been so serious. They were playing with the lives of people who thought they were getting employed.

As I completed my papers, the assistant for Ms. Tames entered the room, and asked me, would there be a problem, if they asked me to come back at another time? I said, yes it would be a problem, and why would Ms. Tames ask me to come in this morning, if she was not going to see me? The assistant then left the office, and came back fifteen minutes later, as I waited to hear the next excuse they would fabricate. I sat there waiting to hear the next excuse, when the assistant came back, and said that Ms. Tames is not here at this time. I knew for a fact, Ms. Tames had not left the facility. For her to leave, she would have had to exit the doorway that I came into, and from where I sat, I could clearly see where Ms. Tames parked her car. I said nothing to assistant and refused to dignify this lie with a response. I decided to leave this place, and debate whether I wanted to deal with individuals that had difficulty with telling the simple truth.

Chapter Four
Dosage of Humiliations

I want back to the facility and subjected myself to the very humiliations as the other clients. Each time a person returned to the facility, they and their bags were searched. Little did I know, that once you developed a good relationship with the security, or support staff, you were allowed you to bring in just about anything whether it was banned or not. In all my time here, I never found it surprising how many illegal items were let into the facility, regardless of how many times administrative staff said it was not allowed. Some clients were also given allowances, by using the side door, and bypassing the search screening process altogether. For example, there is a side door just inside the front entrance, where I saw clients open, and sneak in food, drugs, and alcohol. Many clients even placed various forbidden items inside of their underwear and entered the facility without getting caught.

On other occasions, I saw where foods and beverages were placed into various bags, and security allowed clients to bypass the scanning machines altogether. This happened despite the administrative rules which clearly stated that outside food or beverages are not allowed into the premises.

Placing my leather briefcase in the X-ray machine had become routine for me by now. Me taking my belt off was something I could never get used to. Some female staff liked watching when an attractive male's pants would slip below his waist, and they were able to see things they did not expect. I often saw staff smile and make jokes about seeing a man's unmentionables as his pants slipped further down to an unreasonable level. As I said, I often saw clients stuffing drugs, food, and other contraband inside of their underwear, and security rarely made a fuss. It is because of this lazy mentality that destructive clients made the mistake of thinking various workers were their friends to assist them in unscrupulous activities.

I thought long and hard about whether I should attend the orientation that Ms. Tames invited me to. Days later, I contacted her again and she apologized for not meeting with me previously. In fact, she even allowed me to select the day and time, that we should meet again. I met with my case manager Mr. Baszler, who suggested, that while it was unfortunate for Ms. Tames to stoop to a level of deceit, I may want to see her again, because she is able to get client's paying positions, and no matter what I thought of myself, I was nothing more than a client in the staff's eyes. I agreed that I surely needed one of those jobs about now. I swallowed my pride and focused on bettering my situation. I arranged to meet with Ms. Tames that Monday of all days.

I arrived at the office of Ms. Tames at 9:00 that morning, and to my surprise, she was already in there. She came to the waiting room, and asked me to come with her, and complete my interview. We went to her office, and she took only a few minutes to complete the assessment that other staff had contributed to. We breezed through the preliminary questions such as, why was I homeless, and want I wanted out of her program? I stated that I was here to determine, what her work program, had to offer for a person with my education and experience. I explained my qualifications and stated that her program was geared for assisting those with no high school diploma, and little to no work history, and I was far beyond that. I also stated that her program was geared to assist people with little work or educational history and had a history of incarceration.

Ms. Tames inquired about, how I became homeless, and what have I been doing since I was last employed. I explained that I basically took care of my ninety-three-year-old mother, and I wrote books, screenplays, and various scripts in that time that I lived with her. I explained that I also have two people working on obtaining publishing deals for me. I also said that I wish to get into the television, and movie industries at some point in time. At the sound of hearing that, Ms. Tames eyes grew wider, and saw that I was not to be toyed with or measured against anyone who came before her. She then reiterated that they had a job component that sent resumes to other companies. While I could send out my resume as well as anyone else, I figured, this added component could be worth the trouble of me attending their training. I was told that if I participated in the one-day training, I could then use their client referral services. I was still not satisfied, but I said I would consider utilizing this service anyway. I was then given an admission slip by Ms. Tames and I was set to go.

Ms. Tames lastly tried selling me on her program by saying she had to make sure I was a job ready candidate. I explained that I have over twenty years of high level, social service experience, so I know I am job ready. I also explained that my supervisory experience makes me more qualified than most of her clientele, including her. Ms. Tames reassured me, that once I attended the one-day training, I can go to the company referral services. She then said that her people needed to see whether I could prepare a resume and show that I am worthy of employment. Here I was with twenty plus years of professional high-end work positions, and she wanted to assess my resume writing ability and interview skills. On top of that, this woman had the nerve to say that I needed to demonstrate that I was employable.

I left the program wondering whether I should attend this program, but I decided to reluctantly have a discussion with my case manager. Although I knew far more than what my case manager knew regarding his job, I decided to see what information he was about to give me. We met one evening, and I shared my reluctance on attending what I believed would be a total waste of time. Mr. Baszler tried being political, but even he could see that his arguments for my attending this session were not worth it. He stated that while I may not appear favorable to this orientation, I should attend it anyway, since it was one morning, and according to Ms. Tames, it would allow me to utilize their business connections for possible employment. Despite my apprehensions, I later agreed to attend this orientation.

That Friday morning, I got up early, got dressed, and walked to the employment center. I showed the security guards my pass, and they escorted me to the location where the orientation would take place. Upon seeing me, Ms.

Tames reaction told me that she did not expect me to show up. She greeted me by saying, "Oh, you showed up." That reaction told me that she too knew I had misgivings about attending this orientation. To make matters worse, the training took place in the actual hallway of the training facility. I understood that space is limited but having a training session in a facility's hallway is ridiculous. Ms. Tames then asked, how was I doing today? I informed her, that I felt blessed to be alive. She then said that I had a positive view of life, and more individuals should think that way. I was then walked over to a room that had a piece of white paper hanging on the wall as a background. Ms. Tames took a picture of me with a cell phone and said she would insert it into my file. This should have prepared me, for the level of unprofessionalism, that I was about to face.

The instructor introduced himself, as the director of the employment services. This was the same guy who I saw leading a class by chatting, "We are good. We will be successful," and so on. He then had each client introduce themselves, and ask them to tell everyone, why they were here? He also stated that it was his job to assess, whether those here were employable, and can pass an interview. He also stated that those participating in his weeks of orientation training would decide if clients were ready to be hired or not. I immediately thought this was foolish and idiotic. He also said that he would kick people out of his training if they did not show him the incentive and drive to be employed that he expected. How in the hell could he determine if a person were ready to be hired by this one group meeting? I immediately thought this was too ridiculous and just plain dumb.

I have personally trained people to pass job, housing, and program interviews of all kinds. It was not rocket science to do this. I did it countless times before, and I knew I was good at it. Despite my growing skepticism, I had only a few hours to go before this latest nightmare was over. Right away, the instructor expressed his concerns for three individuals, who he thought were not speaking enough or participating in the group conversations. He even had one client led out of the training by a staff member for what he felt was non-participation. This director found every reason to not be convinced that some clients were not suitable for his so-called training program. He then said something that made me know his real intentions were not to assist clients.

This director stated that his program gets paid for placing clients into jobs, regardless of how long they remain there. So that means, if a client got fired two days after being on a job, his company gets paid regardless. He also said it was his job to find those that can pass an interview right away. To prove that his focus was not on employment, he ended up asking several clients to leave the orientation, and not return. One person said that he wanted to be here because he was a grandfather now and wanted to change his life. This client also said that he wanted to prove he was capable of being a good grandfather, despite not being a good father to his daughter. Despite what this director said, I would have kept this individual and trained him to pass a job interview. That was the kind of motivation that I needed to hear from clients who were looking for a job. As I said, it was not rocket science to train an individual to pass a job interview, or interview of any kind. Given the fact this agency only found low-level jobs for clients, this made it easier to assist clients in getting hired.

At the end of the training, the director said he accepted me regardless of the second thoughts he had about me. I already had my job lined up for the future, and I honestly did not care what he thought about it. I also saw this director stop the orientation and ask his whole staff to meet with him over an apparent disagreement on orientation procedures. If your own staff had major disagreements with your training, then how in the hell can you expect clients to understand what you are trying to do either? I became even more perplexed when it was learned that my training would not be this one morning session, as Ms. Tames had suggested. The director indicated that I also had to complete the full weeks of training under him. I was even more confused when this director said everyone who is accepted, is expected to not allow any outside ventures such as other job interviews, housing pursuits, or educational interest, interfere with their participation in his program. Once I heard that bull, I was ready to leave and never come back. I was clearly told that I only had to attend this one morning of training, and now I found out, that I was lied to again.

I left the facility and did not wait to obtain the certificate that each person who successfully completed the program would receive. My instincts told me that everything this program stood for was a total lie. I could never afford to trust or give them the benefit of the doubt again. I later met with my case manager, to let him know what happened. He shared his true feeling about this so-called training. Mr. Baszler stated that other clients had given him similar reports on this training and those who obtained employment only kept their positions for a few days. He also said this director went against agency protocol by revealing that his agency was getting funding for getting clients employed regardless of how many days, they stayed on the job. Mr. Baszler lastly said that he in all honesty could not blame me for pursuing my intentions of obtaining higher paying positions, because that would immediately give me a way out of the shelter.

As I prepared to leave my case manager's office, he asked whether I wanted him to at least contact the employment agency and get my certificate of completion. I told him that he could do whatever he wanted to do with the certificate, including throwing it away. I simply did not want to waste his time on getting a certificate that I clearly saw, as being worthless. Mr. Baszler took a deep breath, and said he is glad I felt the way I did because he did not want to contact these employment officials anyway. I for one can agree with him on that sentiment. In fact, I should have known that I was in for a negative venture when I asked one of the support workers for the mailing address to the shelter, and they pointed to the hanging shelter sign that said *212 Hades Boulevard*. I found it curious that such an address could easily refer to hell, as a place in which to reside.

Chapter Five
Looking for Reasons to Remain Hopeful

While I viewed the latest vocational pursuit as another waste of time, I did not allow that to deter me from looking for immediate employment. I did not have an internet connection at the shelter, so I did what I regularly do in cases like this. I went to the neighborhood public library with my laptop and used their Wi-Fi connections. I must have sent my resume out to at least twenty-five or more job sites per day. Many of these jobs had lower salaries than what I thought I would ever have to work for again. Because of my situation, I was in dire needs to obtain income at all costs. I nevertheless remained hopeful, that something positive would occur more sooner than later. I began to hope that those that could help change my situation would appear at any day. In fact, one of the individuals that I had high hopes for was my friend and book agent. He was scheduled to arrive in New York toward the end of the month to help promote a movie, in which I gave my input too. Although I had not heard from him yet, I still had hopes that he would contact me with some major good news sooner or later.

Despite not hearing from him or my other major sources, I remained hopeful that he would soon be here. While I waited for news from my high-end source, I was encouraged by new and positive members, who were in the shelter. One such person is a client named Andrew. Andrew and I became friends after entering the shelter and eventually being transferred to where we reside at this same facility. Andrew entered the shelter system about a month before I did. During our interaction, it was as if we were destined to become friends. Like me, Andrew does not have a criminal record, and we always valued higher education. While I majored in music and graduated from Long Island University, Andrew received his master's degree in music from Julliard. We often talked about various pursuits we wanted to attain. One of the reasons for our friendship, was the fact that we both knew that we had to remain focused and not allow the criminal mindset of so many to stop us from attaining our dreams.

While we lived amongst the multitude of criminals, alcoholics, dope fiends, and mentally ill people, we both found reasons to like and respect one another. Although we seemed like an odd pairing for an African American and a Caucasian Jewish individual, we had such a friendship despite the differences of opinions we had. Andrew told me that he loved education, music, and teaching. He also said he is basically one of the best upright bass players in the city of New York. My initial reaction was to think Andrew might be stanching this story a little bit, until he went on to tell me about all the concert halls, and television shows he appeared in around the world. Andrew also said that not only had he played with some of the best musicians in the business, but he also played with some of the most well-known entertainers in the world. He and I used to talk for hours about some of the greatest entertainers in the business. He also stated that he still had the recordings of music to prove it.

Listening to Andrew was like listening to a teacher who not only knew his material but was also knowledgeable in getting his students to learn that material. That is what I believe is the makings of a good instructor. It is not enough to for a teacher to know his material. I have had instructors in the past who knew their stuff but were not able to get most of their students to learn it. This I believe is a major flaw in teachers at the school systems of today. That is the quality that Andrew believed in as well. Andrew used to tutor students in all aspects of music, and he often stated, that if he did not get the student to learn and better understand the material, then he failed as well. Throughout my years of study, I found that instructors that had this quality were exceptional and valuable.

Of all the subjects we debated, one of our biggest agreements came from our belief that family members can become as vicious, and spiteful as anyone. We both believed that such individuals could become as sleazy, spiteful, and unforgiving if the circumstances were right. Andrew revealed an experience he had with his family that caused him to be in the shelter system. Due to illness, operations, and an inability to walk, Andrew was bedridden for years. With only his wife to care for him, this lasted until his mother and his wife eventually passed away. Upon leaving the hospital, Andrew was greeted with an eviction notice from his siblings, demanding that he leave his mother's apartment after years of caring for his elderly mother. I shared the story of how I was treated by my siblings but this story I could also never imagine in a million years. This action can especially happen when an elderly mother is involved. After learning of this story, I found it hard to believe that Andrew could not hold any animosity toward his family members. I then learned that the love of his wife played a great deal in his perception of the world today. Andrew preaches love for his fellow beings, although he chooses to no longer have anything to do with the family that betrayed him.

It was our sharing thoughts about subjects like this, which made living in a vastly mismanaged shelter system remotely possible. We often talked about the many incidents which made us believe that no staff here could help us in any capacity. We often joked about how a lack of professionalism and knowledge was demonstrated by the staff was widespread throughout the agency. Andrew once told me that his case manager met with him and did not understand what a passport was. This is the very woman who was also a supervisor, and did not know what a passport was used for? I also informed Andrew of Ms. Tames lying to me, and my case manager suggesting that I apply for SSI benefits. This person had no knowledge what the requirements to obtain social security were. A last year high school student and a beginning college student would know that a person had to have a mental, or a physical illness to obtain an access one diagnosis to get such benefits. Andrew topped me by stating that his case manager did not even know what an SSI award letter was. The stories that would determine who was most incompetent lives on.

Andrew and I regularly compared stories of staff's great incompetence.

Another person that I had high hopes for is a client at the facility named Bryant. For some reason, I always admired Bryant from the first time that I met him. Although he appeared a bit disheveled, I attributed that to his having lived a hard life of drinking and getting high. I soon learned that Bryant once had positions as a computer programmer, and a maintenance person with the parks department. Our first real conversation happened the day; Ms. Tames came to the shelter where I was. As stated, Ms. Tames wanted to discuss her company's vocational trainings. Ms. Tames even asked was there anyone within the audience, who needs a job? I clearly remember how Bryant was the only person who stood up and said that he needs, and wants, a job and a new start. After hearing the dialogue from Ms. Tames, Bryant was sold and signed up for the security training.

I had a long talk with Bryant, and discussed why he was interested in such training? Bryant confided in me that he worked other jobs including some of the positions that Ms. Tames mentioned. Bryant stated that he also worked for years as a caterer and ruined that for himself by drinking and getting high all the time. Bryant said that he had been looking for a way to get a fresh start and he wanted to take advantage of this opportunity. Bryant was pleased that Ms. Tames said her program would accept, and train him without any specific work experience, even though he had plenty of it. Up to that time, Bryant was a new and motivated man. He began the training that Friday and there was no disheveled look about him. Bryant had his clipboard and pens for taking notes and keeping track of important information. A couple of days later, I was told that Bryant was dismissed from the program because the director and staff did not think he was a suitable enough candidate.

I asked Bryant, why did he feel he was dismissed from the training? Bryant's exact words were that the whole training was bull. Bryant stated that the instructor first had an issue with his not smiling enough, and then the instructor dismissed him for coming late for a session one day. Bryant also said that he saw two females coming late to the class that very day and they started to not go into the class, because they learned that Bryant was treated unfairly. Bryant talked them into going to the class anyway, and they were accepted and graduated despite entering the class later than Bryant. At their graduation speech, they thanked Bryant for making them go to the class even though he was unfairly treated. Bryant had the drive, motivation, and determination to succeed. Anyone with real training could have taught him to be an ideal candidate for employment. I used to be a security guard at one time, and it is not rocket science to train someone. I passionately believe Ms. Tames and the director had no intention of seeing that Bryant made it through that program. I believe that those connected to the vocational program only wanted Bryant to sign up for to training so they could be reimbursed financially once his assessments were complete.

Once Bryant was dismissed from the program, I believe he simply gave up on life. He no longer talked about having another chance to make his existence any better than it already was. He began to hang out with the people that used every kind of drug imaginable. Bryant stopped caring about his appearance. He routinely slept in his clothing, and his original disheveled look reappeared. I tried talking to him about making his life better and not give up, but he had already decided that his life was already what it was going to be. Bryant felt that there was no use in wasting time trying to get something that he was sure will never arrive. While he may have given up hope for himself, I will continue to urge him to avoid those who do not have his best interest in mind and assist him in getting high. This also includes the very staff that is supposed to be servicing him.

I recently got to know someone, who I thought was serious about his life. Winston used to wear the kind of T-shirts that painters in the union wore. I assumed that he knew a little about painting, or he might have someone in his family that knew something about this field. We struck up a conversation when I heard him voicing his complaint, on why it was wrong, for workers to be painting a shelter floor on such a hot day. Winston explained that he was a professional painter for almost twelve years, and his father had painting experience that far exceeded his. The weather was hot and muggy, and Winston knew immediately that the paint job workers were doing would normally take at least two days to dry. Since clients had to be in bed in only a few hours, it did not make sense to paint such a floor under those conditions. As staff considered the options they had to deal with this issue, Winston came up with a solution.

Winston informed shelter supervisors that they had to find professional blowers, and strategically place them around the paint perimeter so the paint would be dry enough for clients to be able to go to bed any time soon. As the day went on, the sound of blowers was still on even after bedtime. Clients were huddled into the cafeteria well past the time, the lights were supposed to be turned off. The next day, I spoke with Winston about how he knew that the paint would take so long to dry? Winston informed me that he learned to paint from his father, who was a licensed painter for more than twenty-five years. Winston went on to say that his father taught him the paint trade and he too eventually became a licensed painter. Winston said that he hopes to get back on his feet with a little help from the shelter staff. I commended Wilson on his having licensed trade experience that he could parlay into helping him get out of the shelter.

I stated that Winston could even investigate city and state positions that hired licensed painters. Winston informed me that his father also had connections he could still utilize for him. Winston appeared so motivated to use his tools to get out of the shelter. He continued with how he knew more about painting than anyone within the shelter system. I told him how proud I was that he remained focused and determined to get out of this shelter. Since then, I watched Winston every day, and I encouraged him to keep motivated and get out of the shelter system. I then began to see something about Winston that I did not like, or respect at all. There is a saying that parents told their children when they reach a certain age of possible danger. The phase went, show me your friends, and I will tell you who you are. This warning meant that if you associated with those that were not good for you, their negative ways would engulf and easily infect you like a cancer infecting healthy body parts.

I began to see Winston interacting with a client, whose every word had to do with stealing something or breaking into someone's car trunk. As I said before, I did not know who this client was, but I knew a multitude of people like him. It was not long before I figured out his game. Just like some clients sold weed and some sold crack or Y2k, this guy's specialty was obtaining heroin. I tried speaking with Winston, but he began to avoid me altogether. One by one, clients began to tell stories about Winston and how he was now hooked on a substance; that, I knew, would not allow him to stop on his own. I was eating breakfast one morning, and I saw Winston and the heroin dealer talking about a place where they could go make a score. I sat their pretending not to notice them, as Winston stood in place doing the dope fiend lean. For those who do not know what that is it is when a person is so intoxicated, and ready to fall, but all their strength is used to hold them up, no matter how low they get to the ground. Winston refused to move from the very spot where he was despite the drug dealer trying to urge him to go someplace with him.

Winston stood against a pole for hours, until security guards entered the cafeteria. The guards showed up three at a time and they were in no playful mood. The commander looked at Winston, and said, "Damn, not this BS again." Winston suddenly tried to appear coherent, as he said that he did not want to go to the hospital. The commander told Winston that the ambulance was right outside, and he was tired of seeing Winston doing the dope fiend lean. Winston pleaded to not be taken to the hospital. The commander then said that if Winston falls on the floor, he is to be taken to the hospital, no questions asked. Winston then sat down but quickly disappeared for the rest of the day. Winston's heroin dealer naturally made himself scarce when the officers came around. To this day, Winston has not stopped his addiction. I eventually began to see Winston as another lost cause that had everything he needed to get ahead as a licensed painter but chose to ignore it.

The hopes I had for Winston, had now disappeared. There was no way that Winston was about to stop his drug use without the help of an in-patient treatment program. This I believe is the biggest fault of the shelter system. Even when a substance abuser is identified, absolutely nothing is done about it. The case managers, housing specialist, security, and supervisors, do not know a damn thing about handling these situations. As much as I despised the shelter system, I now wish, I had the power to implement actions that I have seen make tangible results possible. I had a way of forcing even the most resistant client into treatment. I also would never assist any client find housing if he is an active drug user. As terrible as it might sound, the actions I would implement would bring positive results, and save lives. The only thing I could unfortunately do now is pray for those that need help.

Chapter Six
Flippant Reality

During my time of being a client, I had seen enough interactions to know that the attitudes between both staff and client have grown increasingly confrontational. It now seems that such resentment has grown from petty arguments to an actual dislike and despising of one another. While it was rare that I totally disliked any client that I came across, it surprised me of how many of shelter staff had clients they simply tolerated and, in some cases, could not stand. Reasons for this mutual discontent can be from several factors. Clients who maintained their ignorant jailhouse mentality is one of the reasons for this, while workers who compromised themselves by giving into clients demands and not enforcing regulations can be another. I have seen favorable clients cut the line at dinner time and receive their food ahead of those that were initially in line. I have also seen clients receive extra food while others are routinely denied. Clients that complained of this mistreatment are simply ignored and left to complain to any clients who would listen. From what I witnessed there is no real way for clients or staff to address this issue.

One Sunday, I managed to get excess to an electrical socket and plug my laptop in to recharge it. These outlets can be difficult to get to because of the many clients who have personal cellphones, wheelchairs, and radio devices they recharge constantly. In fact, some clients try to monopolize these sockets and use them as their personal plugs, but other clients and staff complaints put a stop to that. In fact, one client tried making money by giving people haircuts in the cafeteria during non-eating hours. This very client not only cut another's hair, but he also refused to clean up the cut hair that were now on the bench he used. There was even client's hair on the cafeteria floor that upset the other clients who had to eat where the cut hair was left.

Administration officials made announcements against this practice but as soon as it was stopped, it was quickly reinstituted, despite it being against shelter rules. Unsanitary haircuts were given in just about every area, especially if money was involved. Just as some clients sold loose cigarettes, stolen items, and other merchandise, clients made extra cash by giving haircuts despite the opposition against it. Some even gave haircuts with the blessings of security guards, and support staff. Because certain staff condoned this and other practices, I felt this would never stop. As I continued to type and use my laptop that day, a client, who had psychiatric issues, tried antagonizing a female security guard, by singing a song he made up, that had vulgar, and sexually explicit lyrics. This client's incoherent verses went on until a male security officer instructed this client to shut the hell up and leave the cafeteria. I even found myself involved in one of these unprovoked incidents recently.

I returned from the public library one day, and I went upstairs to place my laptop into my locker. My locker was on the far side of the room, by the window. The room had those huge mental fans bolted to the walls, to circulate cool air during the warmer months. The fans normally turned slightly from one angle to another to circulate air. The fan that was closet to me was defective and would not turn from left to right. A shelter supportive worker tried repairing the fan, and it was obvious that he did not know what he was doing. When I returned later, the fan was still on, but the front grading was lying on the floor. Several clients complained about this and even voiced their concern that I report this incident; they sensed the supervisory staff was not listening to them. Despite the complaints of the ex-offenders, this was an accident waiting to happen. It did not matter whether this supervisor had issues with the parolees. It was still her job to address this dangerous condition.

I totally agreed with the other clients and went to two supervisors and explained my concerns. After discussing the issue with a female supervisor, she stated that she was aware of the situation, and someone would be coming upstairs to take care of the matter. When no workers came to service this dangerous situation, a client on the floor with mechanical knowledge placed the grading back on the fan. Later in the day, the very support worker tried taking the down the fan to repair it when it needed no repairs to it. The worker took the front grading off the fan and used parts from a second defective fan to possibly make the repair to the first one. The worker was now trying to repair two fans at once. To make a long story short, the grinding from a fan popped open and fell unto the worker and put a deep gash unto the worker's head. As blood streamed from the employee's wound, there were now two fans that were taken out of commission. Days later, a totally new fan was brought by shelter officials to replace the fan that injured the employee. It would have been easier to have gotten a new fan in the first place.

I quickly learned of other problems that are related to these very support workers. Such staff are often given duties they are simply not qualified to do. Such duties include manning the laundry room and doing the clients laundry. Clients often complained of having their belongings stolen, discolored, or even shrunk beyond the ability to wear them. Workers will also retaliate against clients by refusing to do their laundry by pretending they did not have enough time to complete this task. I too was the subject of such retaliation by support workers. I know of clients who voiced their concerns about support staff stealing clothing from clients. I know this is true because I have had clothing stolen from me as well. This was done when clients were off the wards and only support staff was present to clean the facility. I believe this is another reason why such hostilities remain between clients and staff.

One other important issue has to do with support staff substituting as kitchen staff. Such workers are one day doing cleaning and maintenance one minute and preparing and serving client food the next. My experience as a caterer makes me know that this is unsanitary. I also fail to see how some stuff can go from emptying garbage cans one minute to serving client food the next. I have seen this done on more than one occasion. I have also seen staff withholding or selectively giving out certain food items to clients they preferred or did special favors for them. I do not believe anyone should be given special food items based upon their relationship to workers. I too have been told that certain food items would not be given to clients, but when it came to eat, the more desirable items were suddenly given to those who were on good terms with these workers. In fact, I have had workers serving the food question me about why I had come to eat, when I normally did not eat shelter dinners? My response was that whether I ate regularly or not, the shelter is obligated to provide me with a meal.

I often hear workers complaining to one another about what duties they are told to do by supervisors, but they refuse to do it. This I believe is the biggest reason why I think resentments between clients and staff exists. Some clients get to see case managers regularly, while others have gone months at a time with not seeing workers. One client mentioned that he has not seen a worker in several months. Not that he was expecting to be helped with getting an apartment or anything, but this shows the, *I do not give a damn attitude* of the workers here. Another client mentioned that in June, he was told that he would not be getting a housing award letter because he is on public assistance, but that following September, the shelter gave him an award letter that was dated for June, three months earlier than he received it. This client believes that shelter staff purposefully withheld his support letter. I do not believe that all workers are bad, but there are some devious, evil, and corrupt workers who are bold enough to do such things. In fact, a supervisor even recently made the announcement that client mail deliveries will be posted each day because clients have not been receiving their mail regularly and too many complaints have been made against staff.

I was entering the facility and put my bag with my laptop in the bin to go into the scanner. There were four officers around the scanner. I normally place my phone on top of the scanner where the officers were standing. I then let my belongings go through the scanner. I then walked through the body scanning device, that people walked through. This whole process took less than ten seconds. I then went to retrieve my phone, and it was gone. I asked the officers, where the phone that I placed on top of the scanner was? They all claimed they did not see it. No other clients were around them, and no clients would have attempted to steal it with all these officers present. Another reason why a client would not do this is because they were all on parole and would not risk going back to prison for such a trivial action with guards witnessing their crime. I saw the look in the officer's eyes, and knew they were lying about not seeing my phone. I asked one of the officers, that if a dark blue phone turned up, he should return it to me. I then went to the first-floor dormitory to visit my friend Andrew. As I told Andrew about the phone incident, one of the same officers brought my phone to me.

Without saying a word, I took the phone, and went to the cafeteria. I saw one of the other support workers that I trusted, and I told him about the cell phone incident. This worker went ballistic, and said, this was the same nonsense that happened to another client not long ago. I was now surer than anything that my cell phone was indeed stolen by those officers and returned after they talked it over. I went to by bed to record this incident that I wanted to remember.

It was incidents like this that make it impossible to maintain a positive relationship between staff and clients. The fact such clients are still treated as inmates, by a staff that should not be employed here makes this impossible.

The final laundry room incident that I need to mention has to do with stealing by staff. I needed as many facts as possible and I began to speak with the more rational clients who were not complaining because their food was not hot enough, or the water was too cold. I wanted clients who could give me clear rational facts on why they resented certain staff. One client named Nester gave me the most interesting thoughts on this subject. Nester was known for his cleanliness, and he was always cleaning the floor area by his locker. Nester was on SSD, and he loved wearing nice clothing and shoes. One day I asked Nester about his feelings about the staff that did clients' laundry. Nester may have had a criminal history, but he was not a liar. Nester was a no-nonsense individual, who I knew would give me his true opinion. Nester informed me, that he received some back funds from his SSD payments and used some of his funds to purchase new clothing. Nester stated that he purchased new designer jeans that cost over seventy dollars each. Nester said that he wore these items one time before bringing them to the shelter laundry room. Nester informed me that after his clothing was finished, he picked up his laundry, and noticed that three pairs of his new designer jeans were gone.

I asked Nester if he could describe the laundry room attendant who washed his clothing? Nester informed me, that one of the same individuals, who perform a few duties around the shelter was the one who washed his clothing.

Indecently, clients are not allowed into the laundry room, so the only ones who could have taken Nester's belongings were the very employees, who was responsible for washing them. Nester stated that he even approached this worker about his lost belongings, and the employee became insulted and defensive. Nester was finally told that, if he is not satisfied with the laundry services, he could take his clothing someplace else. Nester stated that he had no doubt this worker was the thief who stole his clothing. Nester stated that he no longer trusted any worker at the shelter anymore because he did not know who to trust. Nester also stated that he believed supervisors would only cover for workers like this if he brought official charges against them. I am positive Nester was right in this assumption. Other clients have informed me of similar stories like this involving their clothing being stolen by staff. As I said, I have also had clothing stolen from me as well. It was during the day of an inspection, when I had a green shirt hanging just outside of my locker door to dry. When I returned, the new shirt was gone. All clients were asked to leave the facility that day for the inspection, so the only ones who had the opportunity to take it were the staff that remained at the facility.

It was as though criminal staff know administrators will look to protect them and accept their word over the words of clients that are, or have been, on parole. Because many clients have mental illness or are current substance abusers make it more plausible their stories will not be believed by such administrators. Well, I for one had no criminal history, mental illness, or substance abuse. My college degree, certifications, and my years of social service experience, as an addiction counselor, intensive case manager, and a case manager, made me vastly more qualified than workers employed at this facility. I can absolutely say that I believed there were those in the employment of the shelter system, who were criminals and who should have been terminated along with the supervisors that protected them.

Chapter Seven
A Unique Perspective

I had just finished my breakfast of instant oatmeal, two kiddie sausages links, and a banana, when a fellow client named Desmond stopped by my table. I have only known Desmond since I arrived at this shelter, but I could clearly see that Desmond was talkative, and was enjoying his new relationship with the Creator. In this short time span, I learned that Desmond was once a drug runner for some of the biggest distributors in the Harlem area. After getting arrested and being in prison for several years, Desmond was released, placed on parole, and altered his life. With the help of his family, and the church, Desmond decided to make what he called a lifesaving change for the better. Desmond chose this path, because it was far better than the alternatives he faced, had he not selected them. Picking between his sober life and leaving drugs alone was a no brainer for him. Choosing his family or risk losing them to his criminal lifestyle was an option he was not ready to make.

In thinking back to his negative behavior, Desmond believed it was dangerous, foolish, and short of attempting suicide. Desmond shared the fact that the more chances he took to please his drug bosses, the more he placed his life in dangerous situations. The more he placed himself in such situations, the larger his rewards would be. Being in the company of people who carried firearms, and would not hesitate to use them on him, if need be, was the routine he had gotten used to. Desmond realized that this action did not reflect a sensible, well-thinking individual, but a selfish imbecilic person who took too many unnecessary chances that could cost him his life. Desmond also realized that he had often taken chances that those who paid him to do such assignments would not have taken themselves. This to Desmond was the ultimate act of foolishness he could think of. It was factors like this, that one day made discussions with his family necessary.

Desmond stated that his family told them that they were not going to go through another period of wondering if he got arrested or killed, every time they heard a police or ambulance siring. Desmond said it was unfair to have his mother placed in such a predicament because of his foolishness. It was in this moment of contemplation that he followed the wish of family members and took part in discussions about God. Even before he was released from prison, he found such discussions inspiring and rewarding to the soul. Desmond stated that eventually, he realized how God saved his life numerous times, even when he was doing his criminal activity. Desmond recounted some of the times he could have been killed being in the drug trade. He believed that only a power with such great love could have saved and enabled himself to develop a totally new outlook on life. After being invited to church, he became a regular attendee and believer.

It is because of this unique perspective that I asked Desmond to give me his assessment on what he felt were some of the issues that needed to be corrected within the shelter system. Desmond paused and stated that one of the biggest problems was the multitude of populations, that were housed together and on the same wards. Desmond felt that those with criminal histories often can relate to others who have been in jail. He felt this can be a good thing, only if each person decided to make the commitment to change their lives for the better. Furthermore, Desmond stated that he could easily connect with others who wanted to continue their drug involvement but that would defeat the purpose of his new commitment. He felt that while he was friendly and respectful to anyone, he maintained a healthy distance from the criminal and illegal actions of those who did, or even thought about, illegal activities.

Desmond believed that too many people with histories of incarcerations, came to the shelter, and quickly fell into the routine of getting high, selling drugs, and not caring anything about making the changes necessary to live more productive lives. Desmond stated that many within the shelter system remained here for years at a time, and simply did not see their lives getting any better than they were. I asked Desmond why did he think so many individuals would not ever obtain suitable housing within the shelter? Desmond stated that you must be able to demonstrate responsibility by saving money and placing it into an account to show staff that they are ready to be responsible. Desmond stated that too many people there spent money just as fast as they received it, and this was why many clients did not leave shelters and had been here for years at a time.

The conversation was going so well that I asked Desmond that if he had the power to make this shelter better, what would he do? Desmond's immediate response was that he would have a separation of the clientele based upon the different needs of people. Desmond said it made absolutely no sense to have psychiatrically impaired clients living with those who could obtain housing. Desmond also said that he would try to eliminate putting substance abusers with those that were mentally sick or those who had no criminal background at all. Desmond also stated that he would absolutely have disabled clients that were blind or in wheelchairs moved to different wards from where they could be taken advantage of or not receive the needed assistance.

My last question to Desmond was, is there anything about the facility that he liked? Without hesitation, Desmond stated that the food was rather good when compared to other places. While I chose to include this response in Desmond's answers regarding the shelter, I feel it is important that I include Desmond's passion for eating shelter food as well. Desmond is often seen taking part in discussing foods that he likes eating and cooking. In fact, Desmond often indulged in various food dishes that his family used to make for him. Just recently, Desmond had a lengthy dialogue about the proper way to cook turkey wings, rice, and gravy. This conversation morphed into a conversation of what he used to make when he lived on his own. In fact, Desmond would be the first to tell you that he loved turkey necks, duck, grits, and just about anything that could be consumed.

I have often seen Desmond sneaking foods into his locker, for later times, when he felt the staff was not paying attention. While I feel it is necessary to include this information as part of Desmond's shelter assessment, I also believe Desmond is correct in his assumptions of analyzing the problematic issues within the shelter system. I was recently eating dinner when I noticed a client named Clarence setting and watching television. Clarence was a person who basically kept to himself, but I knew he was a person of a particular intelligence. I saw how Clarence pretty much kept to himself and had better things to do with his life than to get high. I spoke with Clarence and asked, would he mind if I asked about his feelings on this shelter system and those who work and resided here?

Clarence set up in his chair, and I saw a hidden side of him that I never expected. Clarence stated that he saw a whole lot wrong with the shelter starting with the fact that he was not receiving the kind of assistance that he really needed. Clarence stated that he worked as a stockbroker for years before making a foolish mistake and ending up in prison. Clarence stated that he learned his lesion a long time ago and he planned to resume his position as a stockbroker once he recovered from his back surgery. Clarence felt that while the shelter gave people three meals a day and a place to sleep, no one was owed anything. Clarence stated that he simply could not understand why many within the shelter expected to get something but did not want to do a part in working for it.

Clarence said that he also thought it was wrong for clients to wait on staff to find housing for them. Clarence said waiting around for staff only made a client's stay in a shelter longer. Clarence also saw that the staff of this shelter was too incompetent to assist clients with all their needs. Clarence stated that some clients would not even take it upon themselves to obtain jobs, educate themselves, or get into any good training programs. Clarence said that he unfortunately had met people who simply gave up on life and did not care anymore. To illustrate this point, Clarence mentioned a fellow client he knew, who stated that he had been here for more than six years now. Clarence stated that it was ludicrous that most clients lived from day to day and were not bothered by the fact; they didn't care to get out of this "hellhole" of a place.

I then asked Clarence, why does he think many clients do not want to leave here? Clarence thought about it and then gave the answer that I already knew. Clarence said that not nearly enough was done to help and even force clients into substance abuse treatment. In fact, Clarence stated there were no substance abuse prevention programs within the shelter system. Clarence also stated that many clients fell back into their old way of life by selling drugs, stolen items, or anything else they could sell at the shelter. While some clients were able to obtain positions that brought them money, the bulk of their funds went to smoking weed, using drugs, and wasting it on total nonsense that they did not really need. Clarence also stated that clients buying these ghetto, portable stereos was an absolute waste of money and showed that a person was mistakenly thinking of the shelter as their home.

I informed Clarence that I thought the purpose of a beneficial job was to help people to grow wiser. Clarence stated that he believed that most good jobs focused on helping and developing workers to grow and succeed but not in this environment. Clarence felt that these low-paying jobs were too simple and only helped clients feed their daily addictions. To illustrate this point, I shared my experience with the so-called vocational training program here. Clarence was surprised that I possessed the qualifications that I have, and he could not believe how adversarial the vocational staff was to me. Clarence then concluded that the training staff saw that I would not be here long, and they wanted clients with far less qualifications than I had for many reasons. One of which was to bill their insurance regularly.

As crazy as this appeared, I believe Clarence was correct. Clarence said that he tried speaking with some of the clients, but they often ignored it and allowed vital information to go into one ear, and out of the other. I informed Clarence that what was needed here was a system that I used at my time with social services. Those who got high were routinely drug-tested, and if they continued, they were either sent to in-patient rehabilitation programs, or they were transferred out for non-compliance. Clarence agreed that such a get-tough system was needed here. Clarence's final complaint had to do with the lack of assistance someone in need received. Clarence stated that he had been looking for assistance with his SSD case for the longest, but he was getting nowhere. Clarence stated that he was recently turned down for SSD and he was trying to obtain legal representation but had so far not found it.

I informed Clarence that the true crime in this facility was the fact that many workers did not know how to solve the multitude of client issues including those with social security. I then informed Clarence that his problem was not difficult at all to address. I explained that practically everyone got turned down initially for social security. I explained that I could get him the contact numbers to lawyers that would advise him on his SSD appeal. I have helped many clients receive social security benefits, in the past, so this was nothing new to me. Clarence thanked me for my willingness to assist him. I extended my hand and thanked Clarence for being willing to speak with me about those who are still in need of further assistance.

Chapter Eight
The Night Stalkers

One of the biggest issues I find within the men's shelter system is the increased lack of safety within the dormitory walls, especially at night. There are nights when clients are supposed to be in bed and the bed checks are completed, but the activity for some is just beginning. Hours later, clients began to move throughout the facility with little interference from agency security or staff. While there are safety issues throughout the day, the hazardous environment becomes evil and outright sinister at night. Things you would have never witnessed before suddenly come to light as clear as day. Even though security staff periodically make their way into the many sections of the facility, their routines become predictable and those looking to do their dirt can easily avoid them. Therefore, I believe there are many that are released from prison but have chosen to not be rehabilitated and continue their old way of life.

There are some individuals who for one reason or another will not waste time on becoming educated or rehabilitated. Therefore, I believe some individuals continue to do things that would lead them back to a lifetime of incarceration. It is not because they do not have the knowledge or desire to be better. It is my belief that some simply are set in their ways and do not want to pursue anything other than what they knew since before they got locked up. Do not get me wrong, I have seen individuals on every level who were released to shelters and made changes for the better. I have seen people like client Santana get his degree in prison, remain sober, and work hard to comply with his goals to attain much more than what he has attained so far. Santana also plans to be a major contributor to society. For every person like Santana, I can easily name dozens who are continually looking to scam a system that they were too foolish to not avoid in the first place.

People like this, are constantly looking to get high, or sell their products every chance they can get. I look at a person like James who tries keeping his dirty deeds concealed, especially from me. I will explain this later in the book. James tries to keep his drug dealings and drug use secretive, but I can see through him as if he was a transparent sheet of glass. For many reasons, James thinks that I do not know he is supplying most of the substance abusers within the facility. This is part of the reason why his case manager has not made a face-to-face visit with him in months. Not that I think this is right, but James has played a role in helping staff not want to be bothered with him or his negative lifestyle. If a person pays attention, it is not hard to see the drug dealing activity that goes on.

This is also why James is constantly running to the beckoning calls of those who want to buy drugs from him. I have seen how James allows various visitors to his bed at night and supply them with weed or harder drugs that they want. I have seen, how during television sessions, clients whisper their drug desire in James's ear, and that night, he has the drugs they ordered. To this day, James thinks I do not notice what he is doing but I know the game and can clearly see through him and others. I watched my former brother, who was a heroin dealer, sell this poison to those who made deals with him. I purposefully allow James to think I do not know what is going on, for the sake of my getting more information that I can utilize in this book. Trust me, when I say James thinks he is fooling me, but he is constantly being fooled and you can bet on it.

As stated before, there are several hazards that anyone can be victimized from the mere fact of living in a men's shelter, but none are as parallel as the ignorance of those with a gang mentality, preying on selected individuals. I watched how some individuals greet one another by throwing up the gang signs and signifying who is their honorary brother. I have even seen some staff acknowledge that certain clients are their blood brothers that they look out for. Of all the dangerous hazards within the shelter, few are as dangerous as the hidden activity that takes place in the late night. I have seen grown men who claim to be active fathers, addressing their baby's mother with the derogatory phrase that starts with the letter *B*. I believe there is nothing more dangerous than the fact that grown men are allowed to conduct themselves in a wolfpack mentality and nothing is done about it. I have seen fights before, but these are usually confrontations with another individual. Even these events can be dangerous.

I have seen a client with a broken hand fight in the upstairs dormitory, and security officers never went to stop the confrontation. I purposefully tried to alert the officers, but when I approached one of them, this woman became defensive, and yelled for me to get back, and do not ever try approaching her up close like that again. I quickly yelled that I was not trying to approach her in any particular manner other than to be discreet with the information I wanted to reveal to her. I then told this round person that I was not going to tell her ignorant ass anything now. I then went to another officer and explained that I was only trying to alert this officer to a fight on the ward. The staff thanked me for the information. I then told another support staff about this incident, and he too was upset about the actions of this officer. This is one of many reasons why clients will not give vital information to staff in emergency situations.

I have seen several fist fights while at the shelter, but nothing is more dangerous than when clients attack a lone individual, in a wolf pack mode. I recall an incident that my friend Andrew relayed to me. Andrew resides on the first floor on the dorm that is opposite of the wall to the front entrance. No less than four security officers and at least two supervisors and a host of support workers are on the other side of the wall consistently. It takes less than twenty seconds to walk from the scanners to where the officers are to the first-floor dormitory. Andrew told me about an incident that involved clients in a wolfpack mode, getting retribution on another client. Andrew said he fell asleep about an hour after the final staff bed check was done. Andrew said he was then awakened by the most blood-horrifying screams of a client being attacked.

It seems that gang members decided to attack this one client for giving staff information on another who was sent back to prison. Every client on the floor was awakened as the attack went on. Client, in the dormitory, began to yell and that is when the guards and staff came into the dormitory. As this one client was beaten bloody, the security police questioned the beaten client and others, and that is when they were told specifically which people took part in the attack. The staff called the ambulance and made sure they had their stories straight before the faced their supervisors. Just as guards can lie, falsify documents, and change the response time to their addressing an issue, I am positive this was done to make it seem like they addressed the attack as soon as it happened. I remain skeptical that security guards acted appropriately, because many within the organization are incompetent, unprofessional, and basically, do not give a damn.

There is simply no excuse for security to take twenty minutes to address an attack as this. I have come to the first floor, and have seen guards in chairs, sound asleep, and snoring. I know why it is more than plausible to believe that security took twenty minutes to respond to this emergency, as Andrew said. Once the incident was over, police and other staff collected evidence and questioned other clients who witnessed the incident. I learned that staff allowed the lights to remain on for the rest of the night after that predicament took place. Although some clients were violated by parole for their involvement, this still does not address the major issue of safety within the shelter that officers continued to ignore.

Two other night incidents that come to mind have to do with individuals trying to do well but maintaining a jailhouse mentality that eventually caught up with them.

Both individuals were on parole and managed to obtain low-paying employment through agency connections. When a person has spent years incarcerated, just about any legitimate employment opportunity becomes desirable to them. Had I been in their positions, and had limited work histories, I might have taken such employment too. Melton was a short, stocky individual with a Napoleon complex, but he was liked by clients and staff. I have often heard him mention that he had a daughter that he regularly spoke to by phone. Despite everything else, he was working to maintain his relationship with this young child. For that, I had the biggest respect for him.

Melton was on good terms with the female supervisor who normally conducted the bed checks at night. I saw where she allowed certain clients certain liberties, including Melton. Melton was allowed to basically have two beds and on various floors and this supervisor allowed it. One bed was the regular bed that was assigned to Milton. The other bed was an empty bed and locker that Milton utilized when he wanted to. I could only think of one reason for a client on parole wanting two lockers. One is to hide the contraband that you did not want your parole or other staff to find. Why this was allowed, was beyond my mentality, but it nevertheless was happening in front of other clients and staff.

I was in the cafeteria when Milton confronted a known thief that he believed stole property from his second locker. Milton confronted the individual and a near fist fight almost occurred. Mind you both men are on parole so risked going to jail. Later that night after the bed check was completed, and after a security check was made, Milton again confronted this client at his bed and accused him of stealing his property. Milton also had plenty of back up with him as he confronted this individual. As the fight erupted, the outnumbered client fought back, and eventually managed to get to the stairway and alert the security. Most interesting enough was the fact that this female supervisor who gave Milton the favors did not come upstairs. The outnumbered client was then placed onto a different location within the facility.

Later in the week, it was learned that the outnumbered client accused several people with conducting a gang attack against him. While others are being investigated, Milton, who was still on parole, was violated for his role that was caught on tape in the cafeteria threats he made against another client. I am sure that several others will be violated soon because of this. This incident could have easily been avoided, had Milton, and others, filed charges against the client who he claims stole from him. It was because of the jailhouse mentality that I believe encouraged Milton to sacrifice everything due to his holding fast to this ignorant, jailhouse mentality.

The other incident I wanted to mention had to do with a man named Roberto. Roberto was also on parole and was well-liked by many within the facility. For one reason or another, he always got into near fights with others who challenged or provoked him. Roberto loved boxing and he practiced daily and was not ashamed of showing his skills. For one reason or another, it seems that Roberto was getting into confrontations every week. Despite everything, Roberto was a likable person. I was glad that he finally obtained employment despite it being connected to the shelter program and Ms. Tames. One day, I overheard him saying that his parole officer wanted him to quit the work he was doing. The parole officer probably learned how bogus this training was and wanted his client out of there.

In any case, Roberto was in the shower one night when another client was moved to the floor. Because the lights were out, the new client mistook the bed he was assigned to for Roberto's bed. Because it was dark, this client had no way of knowing he was in the wrong location. Roberto came out of the shower instead of questioning the client about why he was near Roberto's bed and locker; Roberto immediately attacked the guy and bloodied his face. The new client tried to explain that stuff gave him, this locker and bed to use. Roberto ever informed the guy that he was in the wrong location. Roberto continued to challenge the guy to a fight. The client went downstairs, alerted security, which came upstairs immediately.

Roberto tried explaining that he had the right to protect his property. The client explained that the lights were out, and he came to the wrong location. This is a plausible explanation, but Roberto's ignorant jailhouse mentality made things far worse than it had to be. Roberto tried explaining that he was protecting his property, but security was not buying it. They asked Roberto, did he see the blood on the other guy's face? Roberto clung to the excuse that he had a right to protect his property. Finally, the guards told Roberto to put his hands behind his back to be handcuffed. Roberto was bewildered in not understanding why he was being arrested and continued his argument. Finally, Roberto was told to put his hands behind his back, or security would do it for him. What was interesting about this incident was the fact that not one client spoke in Roberto's behalf. Everyone knew that he should not have attacked this client for making a mistake that anyone could have made.

That same night, Roberto was taken to the police station and charged with assault. A few days later, Roberto was formally violated by parole and sent back to prison. Both he and client Milton are now serving their time with new charges pending. This is the result of not being able to let go of negative friends or the sick notion of clinging to an ignorant jailhouse mentality, that includes a wolfpack rule of engagements.

Chapter Nine
Sanctified Resentments

I was never accustomed to every food item that was served in the shelter system, but the fact it gave me nourishment and filled my stomach consistently was a bonus. The diet was not as nutritious as it could have been but if my overall dietary plans of fish and seafood had to be temporarily discarded, then this was a sacrifice I was willing and had to make. I learned not to expect too much from the shelter staff. They had gotten used to clients being on parole and being too afraid to risk staff's complaints to their parole officers. This is one reason why shelter officials treated most clients more harshly and did not want to be bothered with them until it was necessary. I came to this conclusion, because of the way the shelter administrators treated the Catholic staff that served food to clients. Those providing the catered food services should have been treated with a lot more respect by shelter administrators, but they were not. Many rules were put in place to make their jobs more difficult than it should be. If I were a shelter administrator, I would bend over backwards for anyone who does such a favor as this, free of charge.

It became sickening to watch how these Nuns and their staff were not given the respect from shelter administrators they deserved. I am convinced that shelter administrators even acted maliciously against these Nuns to discourage them from coming to the shelter altogether. These Nuns were not allowed to serve their food on the grounds of the shelter areas, despite the large space available. Their dinners had to be served in the neutral parking lot that was just beyond the shelter grounds. When the Nuns came with their food, shelter clients nevertheless met them in an eager and orderly manner. Clients lined up and waited to be served plates of food in the neutral parking lot, in all types of weather. Dodging the various vehicles were not problematic for clients at all. They often separated the lines to create space for incoming, and outgoing vehicles accordingly. Clients then formed the food line again, when traffic was clear.

This was one of the few times, shelter clients acted humanely to one another. They freely helped disabled and blind clients to the head of the food line to eat. As each person received their share of rice, lentil beans, and amazingly baked chicken, they thanked the serving church staff for making their food experience better than what they received at the shelter. At this time, clients congregated outside the shelter grounds to eat and enjoy the food. There were no conflicts, disagreements, or fisticuffs of any kind. Clients often talked about how good the food was, and how they wished the Nuns were allowed onto the shelter grounds. Many even suggested that the church staff should be allowed to serve their food in the shelter cafeteria. Clients including myself felt that this was an outright insult and travesty. Clients freely talked about this as they ate their dinners or the various deserts that were provided by the Nuns. As bad as this treatment appeared to be, clients were constantly told by supervisors that their dining must be kept outside, and they will not be allowed to bring any Nun provided food items into facility.

As strange as it may seem, security and support staff took advantage of these Nun-provided services as well. Me and the other clients saw how staff lined up after the clients and were given the delicious foods the Nuns were providing. Staff and clients joked about how the meals tasted far better than what was being provided by the shelter staff. I for one know my foods and this conclusion was indeed as accurate as can be. I find it interesting how clients would not allow staff threats to prevent them from bringing their snacks into the facility. While cookies and other food goods were taken and confiscated by shelter staff, the same inventive techniques clients used to sneak drugs and other contraband into the facility were often used to sneak food into the facility. The food and snacks given to clients was enough to last at least two days and despite staff's objections, food was regularly brought into the facility. If you had the knowhow, brains, and nerve, you were able to get food through security one way or another.

I found it disheartening that after a while, the Nun services were suddenly no longer being used. After weeks of not hearing from them, Clients speculated about why they were suddenly not visiting anymore. Many clients suspected that the Nuns were upset for some strange reasons and did not want to make this trap anymore. For several weeks, this question was asked of shelter officials; and they responded by saying, they did not know what happened, or they would lie and say that they Nuns just stopped coming. Clients began to question the real reason why these Nuns were not showing up anymore. One Tuesday evening, clients saw the Nun van, driving away from the shelter. Clients found it hard to believe that the Nuns would have come all this way for nothing and not address the clients they helped countless times. Shelter clients began to suspect that administrative staff was up to no good. After some checking and staff confidential input, clients learned that shelter officials informed the Nun that they were no longer welcomed onto the shelter grounds and that the shelter staff could do without their services.

On top of that, shelter administrators ordered that the Nuns presence should no longer be announced to the clients even if the Nuns were within the shelter grounds. One client was even told by a supervisor that the Nuns are not serving food today when they clearly came to do so and frustratingly drove away. On another occasion, the Nuns came to serve food, and shelter supervisors told them that clients had already eaten and were not interested in their food any longer. Clients who saw the Nuns and their parked vehicle quickly complained to shelter staff that they wanted the food these Nuns were providing for them. On top of that, clients had also seen the Nun vehicle parked in their usual spot and ready to serve. Clients quickly informed others and very soon, the whole facility knew the Nuns were outside to serve food. Even the support staff complained to supervisors that the Nuns were providing a service and they should not, and could not, be turned away from completing their mission. This, I believe, is one of the biggest acts of evil and sin imaginable. How in the world can people of God, wanting to feed others, not be allowed better cooperation than what shelter administrators gave them?

In no time at all, clients lined up and received their food and snacks like they have always received them. The shelter supervisors continued to caution clients about bringing food into the facility, but this was only due to throw off suspicion about what they were about to do. The security and support staff did not search clients as thoroughly as they should have done, and freely allowed clients to bring their snacks into the facility. Even the most poorly concealed snacks were let into the facility without question. The shelter staff that normally ate the food provided by the Nuns voiced their complaints as well and acted. They announced that clients could not bring food into the facility, but they nevertheless allowed it. Of course, the shelter staff even managed to receive plates of food to enjoy as well. Since that time, the Nuns were allowed to continue serving their food, accordingly. The staff suddenly began announcing when the Nuns were outside to serve food. Despite all of this, I believe a downright evil was now taking place between the Nuns and shelter administrators.

I do not know if it was a religious matter or the fact that the Nuns are Caucasian, but I firmly believe an act of racial discrimination has taken place and is still taking place. I say that because other church officials regularly visit clients and conduct religious services right on the grounds of the shelter. Not only are these services on shelter grounds but they are conducted in the shelter cafeteria. The same cafeteria that the Nuns are forbidden to use are routinely opened to this other group. Furthermore, these church officials routinely provide clients with bags of snacks, personal items, and all sorts of stuff to eat. As I said, clients are constantly told that the food provided by the Nuns are not allowed onto the premises. This church staff is also allowed to give clients Bibles and prey over them as if they are in church, while no such allowances are given to the Nuns. While the Nuns must park away from the shelter grounds, I and many clients have witnessed when the fact that a different church van is allowed to park inside the gates of the shelter facility. Lastly, this church staff is even allowed to roam throughout the sleeping areas of clients to inform them of the church services that are being conducted.

I have no problems with the church officials utilizing the shelter grounds including the cafeteria, but these same allowances should be made available to the hardworking Nuns, who also wish to service the poor and needy. After contemplating this dilemma, I can draw but one conclusion as to why the Nuns are not given equal services as the church officials of which I spoke about. With all sadness, I feel the Nuns are being discriminated against because of their Caucasian pigmentation and their religion. I do not blame the church officials that are granted the right to be at the shelter, but something is terribly wrong when one religious group is allowed to provide such services, and another is clearly shown that they are not welcomed. For the sake of all that truly need the services and assistance of both groups, I hope this matter is quickly rectified.

Chapter Ten
Bathroom Ventures

I never stopped looking for employment since the time I lost my position. I continued to search for jobs every time I went to the library and beyond that. I then saw an advertisement for the government census positions that were opening. I was particularly interested in such a position because the salary started at twenty-five dollars an hour. This was not what I used to make but it would put me in the range of living comfortably. I planned to apply directly through the state for this position and hoped that I was called. As the deadline approached, I suddenly misplaced, or lost, the telephone number to apply for this position. No one I knew was interested in applying, and many did not want to be bothered. I went to the library, but they had already thrown out the papers that advertised for this position as well.

After not having any luck looking for this advertisement, I then remembered the *help wanted* signs that were posted throughout the shelter residence that were advertising this very position. I recorded the telephone number and intended to make myself available. I needed privacy to make my telephone call, so I decided to go into one of the bathrooms at the shelter. I called the number and then asked for the very extension that the flyer advertised. Strangely enough, this announcement sounded like the announcement that I heard many times in the shelter's work force trainings. I knew this could not be right because the state had employees who processed this information regularly themselves. I found it unusual that state officials were not answering my calls.

I hung the phone up thinking I had to have dialed the wrong number. I redialed, and someone again asked me, what extension did I want? I again gave the exact extension that was on the flyer, and I was transferred to an unknown person who was listed as the contact person for this census position. I decided to at least complete this call and see where it led me. After explaining that I was interested in applying for the census takers position, a female said, she needed some information from me first to make sure I was employee eligible. I heard this nonsense before from agency officials, but I decided to finish the call and see where it led. The caller tried selling me on what they could offer out of work individuals, but I again stated my interest in the census takers position. I recognized that nonsense and purposefully did not give my name.

The woman then asked, where was I located? I gave the name of the shelter where I resided. The woman then stated, I had to come meet with her so she could determine whether I was work eligible. I knew the underhanded tactics of Ms. Tames when I heard it. In that split second, I knew this was all part of the vocational scams of her and her bosses. I avoided further conversation and asked when should I meet with her? She said I could come to her office anytime during the week. After giving me her address, I played along with her and said I would be there that week. Thinking she was speaking to a potential sucker and someone she did not know, Ms. Tames gave me her corny flirtatious nonsense, by stating "I look forward to seeing you, baby." I hung up the telephone and thought, *Ms. Tames, and every administrator involved with the shelter is a con-artist, a fraud, and a liar.* I have seen on several occasions when administrators stoop to flirting with clients to obtain their compliance and later bill their health insurance.

The bathrooms are incidentally another area where unscrupulous behaviors are conducted. As I said, clients normally utilize the facilities to smoke weed but harsher drugs are often used in these areas. On several occasions, I was using the facilities and could hear clients snorting and sniffing heroin, coke, and making the sounds of many addicted people who snort such drugs through their noses. In fact, I have also seen such individuals nodding out in the stalls or in front of their lockers after the bed check is completed. Many of these clients are also involved in methadone maintenance programs but still use the drug of their choice. In fact, one person recently revealed to a follow methadone user that he regularly sniffs heroin regardless of what his program workers think. The clients found it amusing that program staff really think that certain clients are working toward sobriety just because they attend various drug programs.

Some clients are even foolish enough use drugs like Y2K under the noses of shelter officials. It is not hard to determine when a person is intoxicated on such drugs. I have seen clients return to the shelter and they normally do actions they do not normally do. One sixty-five-year-old client named Samuel was in the bathroom stall, taking Y2K. Later, he went to the cafeteria and began dancing wildly. This is normally a quiet and reserved gentleman thinking he was as good a dancer as Michael Jackson. This gentleman jumped around attempted various spins and continued to fall on the floor. Samuel would then get up and continue dancing as if his moves were successful. Clients and staff alike attempted to get Samuel to stop this routine, but they were unsuccessful. You could not convince Samuel that he was not as great a dancer as the entertainer was. This activity continued before security came and stopped Samuel from injuring himself. The client was then taken to the nearest hospital for medical treatment. Samuel returned a day later and did not remember anything about his escapades. I have since seen Samuel high many times and acting like an intoxicated fool yelling out a chicken sound when he is high.

Another case of bathroom intoxicants had to do with a client in his sixties named Green. Green was normally a guy who kept to himself and did not bother anyone. I saw Green as he entered the bathroom with a group of other addicts, during the middle of the night. It was obvious what they were going to do and Green for a mature man, was stupid enough to follow them. I knew Green indulged, but I never expected him to be foolish enough to risk life and limp over the poison he wanted to buy. The next morning, green was seen shadow boxing during the middle of the night. EMS was called because Green would not respond verbally and kept looking off into his own world. Green simply continued to zone out and would not respond to anything that was said to him. Emergency medical services then took

Green to the hospital, where he remained until he sobered up and came out of his stupor.

One particular client I need to speak about is a guy named Manny. Manny was alright with a lot of clients but for many of the wrong reasons. Manny was one of those guys from that shelter that could purchase any drug another client, or potential customer, wanted. One day, I saw Manny speaking to a client Markus. I did not know what they were talking about, but I knew the mannerisms addicts used, when they are looking to get high. I also heard Manny adamantly telling Marcus, he could easily get it for him. Markus kept asking, are you sure you can do that for me? Manny would respond that he would see him within a few hours, and he should not worry. Later that evening, Manny was again seen arguing with another dealer about the fact that he was encroaching on his customer. Manny argued that Markus came to him and that was the only reason why Manny agreed to do this, supposed, one time arrangement. Manny also agreed that he would not bother Markus after completing this one deal.

Later that evening, Marcus met with Manny and received what he ordered. A few hours later, I went to the bathroom and saw Marcus reaching for something that was on top of one of the upper bathroom fixtures. Marcus did not notice that I saw him and other clients place drug paraphernalia on top of these fixtures before. I left and went to bed, but the venture did not end there. Later that night, Marcus was seen looking at the bathroom wall with a blank look on his face. Clients continuously called to Marcus, but he would not answer. Clients tried encouraging Marcus to come to bed but he would not move from that one spot.

Clients came to Marcus and told him, that he needed to come to bed before staff did their client inspections. Later that night, staff found Marcus crying in the bathroom, and unresponsive. Staff immediately had Marcus taken to the hospital, where he remained for two days.

I find it disheartening that such a mature man would indulge in something that is so harmful. As crazy as it sounds, I could understand why Marcus's ex-wife no longer wanted to be involved with him. On top of that, I could see why this woman refuses to allow this client around their young children. Regardless of any excuse an addict can make, this sick and selfish behavior puts his children and family in harm's way. I saw where clients cursed out their children's mother because they did not believe their actions are putting their children at risk. I heard how many clients often referred as these mothers as real bitches, who do not want their children to not know them. This sentiment is widely spread by the men who continue to not know the difference between a grown man and a grown boy. So long as such men continue to not grow mentally, this dilemma will continue.

As quiet as it has kept, the aspect of homosexual behavior is regularly spread throughout segments of the men's shelter. In fact, on occasions, such activity is interrupted by staff and other clients. I do not look down upon anyone's behavior. What two consenting adults do in their spare time is their business. However, in a shelter system, I do not believe anyone has the right to bring this activity around other clients. I remember going to the bathroom in the middle of the night and seeing two clients who finished indulging one another in the shower stall.

They were surprised at my seeing them and one even asked if I could keep this matter confidential. I told them that they should be careful enough and not risk such behaviors in the shelter. One sure way to tell that sexual activity occurs at the shelter is the fact that used condoms are often found throughout the facility. I also knew of two other gentlemen that indulged one another regularly and were found in bed together. Security was not as discreet as I was about this incident. The men were told in no uncertain terms that they would either cease this behavior or face possible transfers out of the facility.

Regardless of whether these actions continued or not, I believe that nothing will completely stop this activity. There are simply too many places for dirty deeds to be done, and the bathroom is one of many places, that is not off limits to such individuals. For the sake of all clients, I hope enough is done to prevent such deeds from happening.

Chapter Eleven
Pretentious Friendships

Traveling to the men's homeless facility can be one exceptional venture. The train station everyone has to maneuver is located on one of the notorious places in New York City. As you exit the station, the area is filled with dealers, drug users, and those taking methadone and drugs of every kind. It is no secret that this area is known as *Zombie Land*. Homeless individuals, that have become future occupants of shelters, occupy this area. They ask for donations from anyone that is foolish enough to help them supply their habit. You can easily find the homeless sleeping on the sidewalks throughout this area, and those who often have clothing that is filthy as though they do not wash or change. As crazy as it sounds, many of them even walk around the area without shoes on their feet. The proliferation of Y2K or synthetic marijuana is as dangerous and mind altering as anything out there. I have seen many clients by this product continuously. One client was so high, he ran into the street and went head first into the windshield of a speeding cab.

Another issue that this area is famous for is the male and female prostitution that goes on here. People wearing scantily dressed outfits and hideous wigs approach strangers and regular customers alike in the hopes of obtaining their drug money. Fights of all kinds usually break out over conflicts of who is stealing business from one or another. One addict walked throughout this area selling headphones that he steals and needs to get rid of. This guy says the headphones cost fifteen dollars, but he is willing to sell them for five dollars each. His lowered price was also due to policemen patrolling this area and he hoped, he would not have to be questioned on his sudden supply of reduced items. Many items are normally sold in this area, but most items sold are overwhelmingly illicit drugs, prescription drugs like OxyContin, Xanax, and other hard to get items.

Even the Methadone programs that are sprinkled throughout the area have their share of people who look for bargains to buy or sell anything at a profit. The schemes are ongoing and continuous. This is one area where I continuously see clients from the shelter, buying, and selling their drugs of all types. In fact, one of the major shelter thieves is a guy named Walter, who is often doing business in this area. In fact, I have also seen Walther and another dope fiend client named Jay, doing their usual illicit deals in this area. Walter is absolutely one of the more profitable thieves in the shelter. He goes to large department stores, and shop lift various items, and then sells them to clients at the shelter. It was here that made me think of them many false friendships that in places like this.

As I said, one of the more egregious incidents I have seen at the men's shelter is the constant developing of false friendships. I was never one to develop or need a crowd of friends to be comfortable. In fact, I believe the number of true friends a person will have in their life can be counted on one hand. The kinds of friendships I am talking about are the true friends that will be in a person's life, no matter what. The relationships within clients at the men's shelter are mostly simple, selfish, and self-rewarding. Clients within the shelter system fall into a trap that keeps them from progressing out of the loop of future incarceration and shelter systems.

I know of a client named Davis, who I think has the potential to truly be anything that wants to become. Davis on the one hand prays and reads religious books often. On the other head, Davis smokes weed like it is going out of style and his associations include others who smoke weed, get high, and chose criminal behavior that will surely get them caught sooner or later. Many of these individuals have intentions of imitating the next big drug dealers throughout the city. I often heard client Davis talk about the deals he is making and only needs to be setup at the right location to be even more successful. Davis often gets around the shelter soda machine and pulls out a roll of singles that he hopes to impress other clients looking to be like him. I recently saw something that solidified my coming to this conclusion. Davis was in conversation with client named Jay, who was readmitted after another failed attempt at having his own apartment.

Clients do not normally discuss drug issues around me but because I was laying on my bed and out of visible eyesight, they felt comfortable in talking. Jay was a straight up junkie on methadone and often smoked weed and used heroin. Jay had his vise for heroin, and this told me exactly what he was. Jay also did his dirt outside of the shelter. In fact, he even had possession of a vehicle that he parked just off the shelter grounds. Jay was recently readmitted into shelter after being discharged a few weeks ago. It seems his plan did not turn out as well as he thought it would. Since then, he was evicted and quickly returned to the shelter. In fact, there were a few clients that lived in the facility that owned motor vehicles of their own. As crazy as this may be, they chose to keep their vehicles even if it meant losing their place of residence.

I listened as Jay attempted to give Davis advice on making money by selling drugs he could obtain. I heard how Jay said that once Davis obtained the products, he could help him get it into the shelter facility and make constant sales to any clients who wanted it. These two talked about making the shelter their home base with limitless selling potential. I knew Jay was a dope fiend who would spend more time in jail, but I lost all hope for Davis. He hooked up with another drug using person that did not have his best interest at heart. I recalled how Davis became angry when he could no longer see his child but if he is doing such activity, anyone would understand why the child's mother would not bother with him.

Some of you heard me mention a client named James who was trying to get on my good side. It seems that James found out that I was a writer who expects me to obtain a large sum of income. Since then, James and others have gone out of their way to develop a friendship with me. James constantly comes to shake my hand when he leaves or enters the facility. James even offered me a bread new pair of casual shoes that he says happens to be in my size.

No matter what James does, I plan to keep him at a distance as well. He continues to hope that such a bond would develop between us, but I do not see that ever happening. While people like Davis and James continue their indulgence in drugs, nothing positive will ever become of it, and I will have nothing to do with them. I only wish that their disturbing ventures would one day stop.

Chapter Twelve
From Dangerous to Damaged

I was sitting in the cafeteria when I noticed a shorter, muscular man sitting alone at a table. After noticing him for several days, I saw how even the most hardened clients on parole avoided him and gave him a clear path. This man rarely said anything and never bothered anyone. I found it odd that he one day moved to the floor where I resided, and his bed was just along the opposite side of the wall where my bed was. One of the pleasing aspects of this gentleman was the fact that even the negative staff and administrators had a genuine resentment toward him that bordered on the realm of dislike. I watched this behavior for a few days, to make sure I was not imagining things and I was right all along. There were many staff except a few who disliked him for one reason or another. No matter how hard I tried, I just could not figure out why he was disliked so many people. Clients disliking a person is common for a number of reasons, but many staff resenting clients is not only uncommon, but in my opinion, unprofessional.

One of the most appealing traits of this client was the fact that he did not appear to get high or interact with the criminal element within the shelter. I knew that multitude of substance abusers in the complex so anyone who stayed sober, I took a liking to. I made it a point to get to know this person the first chance I got. One morning, I was getting dressed to get something to eat and we made eye contact. I greeted him with a polite greeting, and he responded in kind. He then asked if I were going downstairs to get something to eat? I let him know that I was, and he asked would I mind having some company because he needed to speak to me about something. This, of course, took me by surprise and made me curious about what he had to say. I told him that I would like some company anyway so we could talk while we ate. A few minutes later, we were in line receiving our rations of powered eggs make believe France toast and containers of yogurt. For good measure, I always had my daily cup of tea. I figured that not even the kitchen staff or their incompetent staff helpers could mess up the tea. They only had to supply the hot water, sugar, and tea bags.

My new acquaintance and I walked to the isolated table where he normally sat. It was not hard to notice, that many other clients, while interacting with one another, kept a curious eye on us as well. As we sat down, my new friend Uri introduced himself, and said that he heard me interviewing other clients for a project and he was curious about what I was writing. Once I told him, he asked if I needed more people for the interview? I explained that while I had most of the people I needed, I would like to interview him as well. I also said that if I am successful, I would give all that I interviewed a cash bonus. I also explained that I was curious to see if it were possible for males in particular situations to receive the help, they may need or supposed to receive. Uri paused for a few seconds and then said that he would like to be interviewed for the book I was writing. Uri agreed to my terms, and immediately began to talk.

Uri stated that he was born in Jamaica and is one of eight children. Uri said he came to the Bronx, New York, at eight years of age. Uri said, his father and mother broke up when he was around that age, and he never was able to get back on track. Uri had older sisters and brothers but some of them lived a bad life as well. Uri admits that he messed up in school and was sent to prison after doing well in high school. Uri also said he was on the high school wrestling team and is a second-degree black belt in martial arts. This was the reason why no clients at the shelter ever dared fool with him. Uri also stated that it took a while, but he decided to change his life and found religion in the Catholic Church. Uri said his mother was a practicing catholic and he took up the religion as well. It was during this time that his family began to see changes within him.

Uri says he was once a heavy drinker and he realized that one drink led to one more, and another, until he could not stop himself. Before you knew it, Uri would drink a whole case of beer without breaking a sweat. This pattern was only interrupted by his looking for more substances, and it usually followed his indulgence to consume weed. Uri said he loved smoking weed as much as he loved having sex. For years, this became his habitual indulgence to cope with issues that were unsatisfied as a child. Such issues included issue of having attention deficient disorder and seizure conditions that placed him on SSI. Although his mother was his payee, this made Uri feel inadequate and less of a man. As he grew up, Uri never worked a real job before, and felt inferior to others who did have jobs. These feelings even engulfed his owe family members. Not even his being on past wrestling teams could make up for the pain of believing he could never be a man. Before long, Uri made the mistake of selling drugs and weed before landing in prison for that and other offenses.

When Uri was released, he still had issues of that he never came to grips with, that included his father leaving his family and having babies by other women while he was involved with his mother. Uri admits that this anger consumed him to no end. It was not until he was released and joined the church that his life began to change. While Uri admits to still learning better patience and self-control, the fact that he avoids conflicts and physical violence shows how far he has come. I still say he needs to avoid his negatively referring to some women as whores or bitches, but I feel for what he has gone through and the strides he has already made. I genuinely feel that Uri wants to change is life and work to become a responsible sober man. I have no doubt that this is a real possibility he will accomplish in time.

Another person I need to mention is a client I mentioned before named Danny. As I said before, Danny was intelligent in one way but completely dense in others. Danny was diagnosed as having autism as a child and being raised in the foster care system for years before he was adopted. This caused him to face many traumatic and lifelong family issues. For one, Danny has a low self-esteem issue from being overweight and was perceived as dumb. Danny also has issues with not being able to find employment, and some of his views are outright racist. Despite all of that, I refer to him as a worthwhile friend. I also have respect for his willingness to be employed. Danny spent time in prison, and I believe this was due to a sexual incident that involved a female. I assume this view because at one time, I was going to help him apply for a peer counselor's position, and he said he did not want to be a peer counselor. When I asked him why he did not want to apply for any peer counselor's position, he said that he would rather not discuss that issue with me. He has, nevertheless, gone to various mental health programs and clubhouses but none have been able to obtain employment for him.

One of Danny's biggest issues is the fact he thinks he is smarter than anyone that hires him. Danny says he does not believe this, but I have seen him in enough situations to know I am right. A few times, I asked about how his job interview went, and he admitted that he told the interviewers how they could help the workers increase their performances. Even if the suggestions were sound there is some advice that you just do not give at an interview. The last thing and interviewer needs is someone coming to the job and trying to run things their way. Danny never learned and will never learn not to do this simple controlled behavior. Despite the flaws Danny may have, he has a tenacity to pursue suitable employment that goes beyond measure. In fact, I believe Danny has the drive to obtain employment if he could control his giving his personal opinions too much. Very recently he received a referral to the parks department for a job but was declined due to a conflict with the mental health program. Danny was mortified and hurt by this action that a referral program would send him to a place where there was a conflict between the two programs. I suggested that Danny should just not accept program referral and apply to the parks department on his own if it was not too late. Danny is computer literate and could easily apply on his own.

After that, I suddenly noticed that Danny was returning to the shelter well after curfew hours. He tried telling me that he was attending a church function, but I knew of no church function that would cause him to return to the shelter at almost 11:00 pm. Danny's bed was right next to mine, and I noticed he was coming to the shelter late too often. One night, a strange thing happened. I returned to the shelter about 8:30 pm, and a female supervisor stopped me and suddenly asked if I still had a bed? I replied, of course I do. I found that question somewhat odd because this worker never bothered to speak with me at any time. That night, I knew something was going to happen. I was lying in bed after 11:00 pm, and workers came to Danny's locker and cut his lock off. They then took his belongings out of his locker and packed them up for transfer. Most disturbing about this was the fact that the workers voiced pleasure in taking Danny's belongings out of the locker and saying this dude has too much damn stuff in his locker anyway.

Yes, Danny was late, but he was smart enough to call the shelter and let them know he would be returning late, so there was no reason to take his bed and locker from him. I saw Danny that morning after he spent the night in the shelter lobby. He had just been given another bed on the same floor that he was originally moved from. I then remembered the brief conversation the shelter supervisor had with me the night before. I theorized; she had this all planned out to get Danny at any costs. Danny was angry but was content to return to his original floor. Giving the history of the shelter administration, I can see them doing such an underhanded thing to Danny as a show of retaliation. They knew Danny was coming back and they wanted to teach him a lesson. I would not be surprised if they somehow came after me in the future.

The move they made also had a larger motive to it. It showed all clients that no matter what they may think, clients own nothing within the shelter system. Clients can buy all the personal property they want, but everything here belongs to those, who run the public's shelter system or the imitation version of the insane asylum.

Chapter Thirteen
Wishful Thinking

Despite my days in a men's shelter, I believe in the importance of visualization and truly seeing oneself in far better conditions. Despite everything, I can truly see myself leaving the shelter and being in my two or more bedroom condominium. I can also see myself being so successful that I start a housing program for clients that have little chance of obtain stable independent housing on their own or with the help of shelter officials. I know for a fact that many clients do leave and accept private rooms that administrators found for them, but this does not work out promising. Landlords do not waste time on clients in any way. Landlords will quickly evict clients and their roommates for any violations such as drugs and alcohol. Many clients return to the shelter months later without the section eight that agency officials promised them. Men are being fed lies by shelter staff when they are told that section eight vouchers would be there for them once they are discharged from the shelter. Section eight vouchers have priority for mothers with children first and not men. Once this is learnt by men, they will be better off.

I truly envision myself developing a housing residence for such clients that will include my friend Andrew, whom I know has various illnesses and would love a stable home. Another client I would place is my friend Benny who has worked as a painter for years and would gladly help in my efforts to obtain housing and fix them up. Another I would help is my friend John, who was one of the first person that I interviewed. While I suspects he avoids hard drugs, if we could come to an understanding that he abandons weed, I would surely assist him with housing too. I would also assist others like my friend Clearance who does not do drugs. Clearance also attends church regularly and has changed his whole life around. Clearance was also involved in obtaining commercial and residential properties and would be an excellent asset. I would also like to help Santos, an elderly man with illnesses that hinder his mobility. Santos would love to have a place where he could pretty much enjoy the rest of his days be safe and not have to live around the negativity of a homeless shelter.

I would also like to assist my friend named Roy who goes to church and does not do drugs or alcohol of any kind. I would also like to do something for my friend Cheesehead Danny. Cheesehead is not his given name, of course, but I named him that because as smart as he appears to be, he is so dense, and simple. Despite some not liking him, I found Danny to be a good friend. Cheesehead, often talks about wanting a job and having wasted years of life not attaining much. I honesty would have no problem with given him employment if I could. Despite some accusing him as being a racist, I think he could do well with Benny leading a group of painters and fixing up housing. Danny seems like a racist, but I see him as having a little Archie Bunker in him. He also confided in me that he yells so much because he is losing his hearing. Danny also mentions that he has autism and was scorned and ridiculed his whole life. Danny wants to only find employment and work for a living.

I am sure there are others that I would assist if I could but trust me, they are not forgotten. While I also want to surely gain housing for myself, I will continue to pray to the universe that all my special dreams and hopes will come into reality soon. I pray that this book reveals that homelessness is something that could befall anyone and everyone. I pray that wealthier beings learn that it is part of their spiritual obligation to help the homeless live better lives if they want to do so. I pray that people will understand that they should not discard all homeless beings as useless ones who do not want a better life. Do not get me wrong. I firmly understand that some people not only deserve to be in jail but what happens when a personal debt to society is paid. Is it right to continue punishing such a person because they were incarcerated? No one deserves to be continuously punished for a crime they may have committed in their lives. That is exactly what the public shelter system does. There are many homeless people who deserve better than to be forgotten by a shelter system that simply sees them as nothing more than billable pieces. I pray that people understand that homelessness is often a matter of unfortunate and unforeseen circumstances. I pray that people understand that homelessness is often a matter of people falling between two sides of the same coin.

Chapter Fourteen
From Bad to Unreasonably Bad

As I said, there was never a happy day while I was living within a men's shelter. While many clients spent most of their time within the facility only to leave to pick up their drug of choice, I did my normal routine of grabbing my laptop computer and going to the public library to write creative works like books and screenplays. I also used these sessions to continue my efforts to gain employment and obtain the income I needed to get the apartment that I want. It was while I was at the library, when I met another educated client that quickly became an associate of mine. I had seen Lenard using his laptop in the library many times and he one day noticed that I was writing one of my books. He asked was I working on an assignment, and I told him about some of the works I was completing and hoped to soon get published. We then got into a lengthy conversation about writing, and he has been one of my close associates since then.

Before Lenard moved to a shelter not far from where I was, I learned that Lenard used to be a teacher and he also went to various schools for writing screenplays and movie productions. In fact, he also told me about his directing and a short film that he wrote. He did not like the fact that it did not do well but I told him that he should be proud of his accomplishment regardless. Lenard and I became thick as thieves and met just about every day to write and create. He even told me about various places I should submit my scripts to, including several script writing contests. The thing about such contests is that many producers and movie makers can review your work so even if you do not place in the contests, they can still contact you and be interested in your screenplays or books. Even if one still had to come up with the initial admission fee, it was still beneficial to take such contests into consideration. I would have never found such avenues had it not been for Lenard. For that I owe him a special debt.

My friendship with Lenard had become so influential that we met regularly to write various scripts, books, and other creative works. In fact, we also had a friendly rivalry where we discussed potential screenplays and other materials to submit to various competitions of interest. Lenard even entered a major script writing competition in Atlanta and recently received word that he made it to the quarterfinals. As impressive as this is, I jokingly told Lenard that he was lucky I did not have the funds to enter that competition, otherwise, I would have won it. Although we were friends, it was rivalries like this that fueled our friendly competition even with one another.

Lenard was also influential in alerting me to a nearby college venue where we could meet and have free internet access. The college site had restrooms, comfortable tables, and a food facility that we often utilized. We practically lived in this facility and became friends with the staff that often gave us free food. I was not sure they fed us because they knew we were homeless or because they admired our passion for writing despite our unfortunate circumstances. Most important about this site was the fact that it had protective security staff that made sure everything was kept in an orderly fashion. I especially enjoyed this site because it normally opened from 8:00 am to 8:00 pm. The fact that I had twelve hours of uninterrupted creation time was immeasurable. It was because of this site that I was able to create some of the most creative works that I have ever done. I so looked forward to going to this site that it helped take my mind off not having a home and living in a shelter. I still regretted having to return to the shelter before curfew, but it was still gratifying to be away from the shelter for most of the day.

One thing we had to do at the shelter was to sign for our beds every night. As I said earlier, that if a person did not sign for their bed, it was quickly given to someone else who needed a bed. That was one thing that I especially kept in mind. I made sure to always sign for my bed each night. Clients who lost their beds had to sleep on the lobby bench until a bed somehow became available. There were countless times when a bed did not become available until the next day. As uncomfortable as these beds were, I made it my business to never lose a bed for not signing for it. The fact these beds were narrow, uncomfortable, and short, did not stop them from being a hot commodity at the shelter. It was in signing for my bed one night that I received news that would affect my staying at the shelter facility.

One of the few things that went well for me was my recent meeting with the housing director. Since I worked in social services for years, I applied for an early pension, and I received notice that I will receive it. I was also interviewed by the housing director and received notice that I would also receive a housing voucher that includes paying over thirteen hundred per month in rent. My housing package had to be sent to city officials for their approval, but the housing director reassured me that this was only a formality, and I would quickly be approved. I had second thoughts about accepting placement into a city facility, but this voucher would allow me to save my pension for an even better apartment down the line. I figured that since I spent time in a shelter, I may as well get something worthwhile out of my suffering. The housing director admitted that my case was so unusual that I would be approved for just about every housing package that I applied for. The housing director also stated that due to the city being closed because of the coronavirus situation, the city is moving quickly to approve housing packages. Since the housing director already completed and submitted my housing package, this gave me additional hope that my package would be approved quickly, and I would soon have my own apartment.

I had just signed for my bed for the night when a support staff asked me my full name. The staff worker then sorted through a stack of papers until she came to a letter that had my name on it. The letter stated that I would be moved to a hotel in the diamond district the next morning. I was advised to pack my belongings tonight and be ready for transport to my new location between 9:30 and 10:00 the next morning. I believe that such a move was being done to provide services to the many homeless people who slept on trains and in the subway stations. I now see where the ones who are close to leaving the shelter and do not have mental illness, are the ones being moved to a hotel. I may not have the complete rational for moving people out of the shelter, but I know I am on the right track. Even with this shelter move, there are still several individuals that will prove to be undeserving of being moved to a quality hotel. There are simply too many people in the shelter that are on parole, use illicit drugs, and maintain a criminal mentality. In any event, I packed my belongings and waited to be transferred in the morning.

The next morning, I waited to hear when we would be moving to the hotel. After not hearing anything until well after 9:00, a follow client came to our floor, and said he wanted to relay a message from the staff. We were then told that client moves to the perspective hotel would not take place today. Every client was angry at hearing this news. Some clients even took off from their jobs and were told the move would not take place. I for one had a different point of view of this matter. I immediately went to the supervisory staff, and asked, was the move cancelled as a client stated previously? The supervisor informed me that the move was indeed cancelled. I then asked, why were clients told to pack their bags last night, and be ready to move this morning only to have it abruptly cancelled? The supervisor stated that they were not assigned to work last night so they would not know what happened to change the situation. I then asked a supervisor, why was a follow client told to tell clients about the cancellation and not have supervisory staff address the issue? The supervisor again stated that he had just arrived on the job, and he did not know what happened. I then asked the supervisor, who was the supervisor that said the client move was now cancelled. I was then told that this supervisor knew nothing about why this move was now cancelled or which supervisors were informed that this move was cancelled.

I angrily left the facility after not getting a suitable answer. I returned later that afternoon and was shocked when a supervisor told me that the hotel move that was cancelled was now rescheduled for 5:00 pm today. What was scheduled for a morning transport, then an afternoon one, resulted in our getting to the hotel at almost midnight that night. In many ways, staying at the hotel had more positives than negatives for me. I was given a single room while others had to share with a follow client. I had cable and the internet so typing my materials was a blessing in disguise. The negatives were too many to document. One of which was the fact staff would do evening bed checks by knocking on the clients' doors, and abruptly entering to see if a client were in his room or not. This practice only stopped when enough clients complained about having staff violate their privacy. Another issue I experienced was having two-night staff knock on my door during bed checks and telling me that if I am going to smoke marijuana, I should buy some air freshener and use it to prevent the administrators from smelling the marijuana when they came around.

Therefore, I am determined to obtain my apartment and never again utilize a shelter. While I am continuing to document my staying in the shelter system, this experience has been the most tiring I was ever subjected to. This is also an experience that I pray I will never have to repeat. While I intend to go on to bigger and better things, I will never forget the nightmare that I refer to as my time in a homeless shelter. I vow to never forget the period I refer to as *Sides of the Same Coin*.

Others are guilty of this. I know for a fact that some workers had the same vises that many people residing within the shelter facility have. I did not report this latest transgression, but I knew I would record this incident and tell all who would listen about how some shelter officials conducted themselves. I passionately believe this is a large reason why substance abuse is present within the shelter system. Few people here even give a damn.

The number of incidents like this is too many for me to indicate. While some workers were good and wanted clients to do well, others simply did not care one way or the other. It was such incidents that continued to motivate me as much as anything. Every day was a period for me to continue my efforts to get out of this purgatory that was called the shelter system. Every day I exist will be focused on obtaining my place and to write my scripts and books that will enable me to live the life that I want to live. I pray to the Creator of the universe, that I leave this situation that shows the existence of *Sides of the Same Coin*.

The End